TOA

OTHER BOOKS BY THIS AUTHOR

English Language as Hydra Its Impacts on Non-English Language Cultures. Vaughan Rapatahana and Pauline Bunce. Multilingual Matters, U.K. 2012.

Schisms. Stonesthrow Poetry, USA. 2012.

China as Kafka. Kilmog Press, Dunedin. 2012.

She Was No Good Anyway. Good Samaritan Press, Thailand. 2013.

OTHER TITLES FROM ATUANUI PRESS

On Tongan Poetry by 'I. Futa Helu

Waiheathens: voices from a mining town by Mark Derby with paintings by Bob Kerr

TOA

Vaughan Rapatahana

Atuanui Press

ACKNOWLEDGEMENTS:

Kia ora katoa.
Special thanks to Let for letting me thrive and
to Po Lam for input on the cover.

Cover design by Ellen Portch

Published by Atuanui Press
1416 Kaiaua Road
Pokeno 2473
RD3
New Zealand

http://atuanuipress.co.nz
editor@atuanuipress.co.nz

For my son Blake—who died far too young.
Kāore ahau he wareware koe.

ONE

Mahon farted vociferously. Too many fucking meat-pies, semi-heated in roadside garage microwaves. Too much stale draught beer. Too much junk food. Too much of everything. Too much. Too much repetition. He wound down his darkened window to let escape his own fetidness.

Outside the air was spring-fresh. Then, within a few metres, the sickly-sweet stench of new silage blew into his nostrils. He imbibed deeply, his inner regions grasping drunkenly for what the smell echoed. There was a sort of memory ... but he couldn't think what of ... his mind kaleidoscoped and a whirr of psychedelic colours overwhelmed him to the extent that he took his foot off the accelerator pedal and let his Zephyr coast over to the side of the road.

Mahon had been losing his mind for what seemed like years. He tried to keep it reined in, but it kept breaking out like some obscene drunken uncle.

There had been terrible flashes where he had stared at his hands as if they were something hostile and foreign. Disembodied objects. And he wondered if one day they would rear up and throttle him without warning. He wondered what they did when he wasn't looking.

His brain was beyond postmodern interpolation—post-Virilio—post-Internet whizzbang rapidity in a garbled dimensional continuum of its very own. Mahon and his brain were out there, not always in tandem.

The car stood thrumming, not missing a count. Mahon's mind spun, skipping countless synapses, his mighty metal road-carcass charioteering his dysfunctional inner one—itself further layers of an onion—corporeal carting cerebral, ignoring Gilbert Ryle. The car knew more about where he was going than he did.

Mahon, my dear friend, was in a very bad way indeed.

*

Not many knew about the site not far away from where Mahon was now slumped over his steering wheel, and of those that did only a handful really knew what was going on there. Information was as lacking as inmates, who were scattered in cells empty apart from a bare bed, a desk and a chair. Isolated by the current regime as 'terrorists', 'stirrers', 'agent provocateurs'—as identified by the minor but vocal coalition partners, and their cohort of paid snitches.

TE PUNANGA was the cynical sign on the perimeter of the barbed wire enclosure just below the rudimentary guard pavilion, itself kilometres up a dry creek-bed that skulked away at an oblique angle from the remote country road. This was no sanctuary. This was a 'reform' prison—for many a life sentence. There was torture. Blackmail. Threats. Chemical and electrical 'modification'. You name it, all manner of 're-education', even if no such nomenclature had yet been coined.

It was best if men like Mahon didn't know about such a place. He would never have snapped out of his free-fall if he did.

Mind you, Mahon hadn't always been this screwed-up. Once he had been reasonably unscrambled. Sort of poached, maybe, but not heavily fried. OK, maybe not always sunny side up, but reasonably palatable. Once or twice, indeed (or was it more?) Mahon had forgotten and / or suppressed entire episodes from his past, and—worse—had begun to substitute others' life-sagas as his own. A conglomerate of book-creatures and denizens from the big country's moronic movies were now also characters in Mahon's background. Mahon's history had become part mythic. He was living—in some demented fashion—his own and others' fictions. Mahon had been married, 'settled', mowed lawns, watched television and understood what was being purveyed, read magazines and enjoyed them, mowed lawns, gone out to dinner—well, at least to hamburger shops, listened to the radio—especially if it was Classic Hits, bought daily newspapers, mowed lawns—you know the sort of thing. A regular suburban guy. Christ, Mahon was to all intents and purposes 'normal'. He prayed quite sincerely to God reciting the Lord's Prayer before sleep. He never missed, even when pissed. He dared not not make this magical incantation for fear that he would be overlooked on the Day of Judgement. Besides which, he had believed that prayer worked. Especially in desperate situations.

Not any more.

Mahon farted again as he leaned against the side of his car peering at nothing in particular in the paddock. Finally, something resembling common sense leaked into him and he reached through the open car window and turned off the ignition. He spat. His spittle tasted bilious and unpleasant. Gone were the days when he cleaned his teeth methodically morning and evening. Vanished also were those fleeting glimpses of something beyond the diurnal dross. Those epiphanous moments when Mahon became warm and all-knowing—whole. All gone.

He had become passive; played-on. He didn't instigate action anymore, he seemed to sidle into it. No longer a centre-stage actor, merely a sort of extra in his own drama. Reduced to a cameo role in his own fiction for Christ's sake! A fucking stunt double in a B-grade movie. An Eastern movie at that—one of those screaming, dancing, smiling dervishes of a film where every scene is a replay of an earlier one, where every movie is a remake of the one before it. Where every actor is frenzied and feverish.

He spat again. What to do next?

A caustic sweat ran down his forehead. He used his sleeve to wipe it away. The sun was high in the sky bearing down on him. It was hot, he realized for the first time. He was perspiring a lot. Was it that hot though, or was this some physical foreboding? He peered deeper into the paddock, squinting myopically at something he thought was approaching. What was it? Was it anything at all? Or was this another vestige from Mahon's LSD days / daze long-gone?

Questions, questions. Always questions. He wondered WHY he had cartwheeled into his present miserable state. Perhaps he had *OD'ed on life itself*—and here the lyrics of the Blue Oyster Cult song hit him 'and everything had finally gained on him, overtaken him.' Perhaps he was free but bored because of it, here Sartre's 'Man is determined to be free,' fought a losing battle for space in his mushy forebrain. Age had flattened his percipience, stubbed his desires, burnt out his idealism. Was he in fact just an aging, overweight man, flummoxing around trying to escape his own past? Here Ortega's voice sneaked up and bleated, 'Each man is the author of himself,' right in his face. Perhaps the truth hurt him too much.

Mahon looked down as sweat invaded his eyes. When he looked back up, whatever it had been, had gone. The sun continued its torture, he could taste its rays. Mahon's hair—once jet-black, now a sort of mottled gray—was dripping. He ran one of his hands through his bedraggled locks and stroked his beard with his other. What now?

Another car sped by, impersonal. Mahon made

no eye contact—the vehicle could have been driving itself. The dust invaded his eyes, he rubbed them vigorously, squirrels of light sped past his pupils beneath the shuttered lids. Vague semblances of faces appeared and then quickly vanished. Were they independent visages or Mahon's own phenomenological nuances? Was it a duck or was it a rabbit? Was it anything at all?

Upstairs, the sun turned up a few more degrees. Mahon began to broil. He took off his sweater, stretched and yawned. Mahon kept a gun—a rifle, to be exact—under the front seat of his Zephyr. He called it Molly. Molly the gun. He had wanted to kill someone once, but had now forgotten who that might have been and why. He performed a pre-programmed ritual of stroking the rifle, but the gesture was hollow, a mere simulacrum of something that had once made some sort of sense. The shaman had left the building long ago.

It wasn't a sexual simile, as you may well be thinking, no, Mahon stroked the firearm in an effort to draw back meaning into his life. It was as if by performing the routine he would be able to make sense out of the puzzle he was merely a clue in. Via this method he wanted to somehow abnegate his birth, to cease to be what he had become, to glissade into another form entirely. The rifle, quite literally, would be his hand-maiden in this symbiosis.

It was time to go.

TWO

Society had always had institutions of convenience somewhere in the skinny country: the places that we send 'don't-fit-ins' and 'out-and-out criminals' to, when they become too much of a hassle for us. Or because they are just too damned dangerous. We spend millions on locking them up. But TE PUNANGA was different. The ruling oligarchy hadn't even bothered to consult the public about the establishment of a place where people—mainly men—would be stashed away for the sole reason that they had dissented, or were likely to. Most of these inmates had been identified by the growing plethora of informers as wanna-be rebels and radicals, rather than as bona-fide insurgents. The skinny country was rapidly transmogrifying into a third-world cabal of informers, undercover agents and secret police.

Violence, per se, was still more of an ambience than an actuality, but it was just this opaque veneer of promise that empowered. People were incarcerated because they had the potential to 'make trouble'. Cause and effect were all buggered up.

So some people—mainly Indigenous, who after all had the most to gripe about—were simply not around anymore. And given the restrictions of TE PUNANGA they weren't having any success existing there either. On some rustic nights you could hear whimpering from along the corridors, or the occasional testicles-sliding-down-the-razor scream.

Mind you, no one would have dobbed in Mahon, especially in his present parlous state. I guess that's why I still haven't met him, only heard a lot about him from guys in here and out there, and read his works of course.

Still, I am coping most of the time I'm here. I do a lot of writing to fill in the days, weeks, months: even though it gets checked on regularly. I play around with it a lot too, I've got the hours at my disposal. Previously I was always called a bit of a clever dick. Smart arse. Wise guy.

*

Mahon arrived on the outskirts of a typical skinny country village—long grass and stray sheep on the fringes. A few rusty car bodies. A few more up on blocks. A lonely gas station. A dishevelled post office. A solitary church at the end of the hamlet—newspapers and milk crates asleep by the side of the road.

One or two people strolled languidly across the street as Mahon parked in the shadiest place that he could find—outside the pub / hotel. He turned off the engine and sat stupidly for a moment wondering why he was there. The scene could have been from a western movie: the pause before the climatic gun battle. Big Bad Jake strolls into town. An eerie silence pervades. Cats skulk under the verandahs. The few living souls scatter to their hiding places—you know the sort of thing. Mahon half-expected

Joel McCrea or Randolph Scott to appear. His reminiscences may have been lopsided but he could still recall names, especially those of western veterans: filmic or factual.

Then it flicked into his mind—he needed a drink, a cold drink—he was bloody thirsty. He padded over to the dirty side door of the public bar and ambled in. Shit, it was dark in there. Mahon couldn't see anything for a moment. He had to take off his shades, but even then, it took a while to discern any detail. In fact, his first sensation was auditory—he could hear the dull click of snooker balls and what seemed like mumblings from the opposite side of the pub. After a while, and a fair bit of floundering in the gloom, he bumped into the bar. He glided his fingers across the warped, splintered surface and peered again into the murk. The vinyl flakes sprung into his fingers and he flicked brittle pieces towards the floor. No one seemed to be behind the counter.

Yet there was someone around somewhere—he could distinctly hear voices behind him. Men's voices, talking about God only knew what. Mahon waited as patiently as he could, thirst exploding in his throat. His parched larynx finally had to surrender and he rasped out a perfunctory "Hello." Nothing. The voices had faded away now. He drummed his fingers on the counter and thought about going around the other side and helping himself to a drink. So he did. He drew out a cold bottle of beer from the chiller and swilled it down quickly. Good. He began to relax a little. The alcohol percolated down, down, down, and suddenly, Mahon knew that he had been here once before. Maybe in a dream ... A dwarf's voice spoke up. It was saying, "That's five dollars, mate". The dwarf had seen Mahon steal the cold bottle and wanted reimbursement. Mahon was startled to say the least. Mahon had seen dwarves performing in a circus long, long ago and knew they were agile little buggers. Not to be crossed—hard little men—especially those who had been victims of throwing competitions so liked in the backwoods of the big country. He rummaged in his ratty pockets for money and slapped five dollars down on the bar.

Then he asked for another bottle. He guzzled and began to feel quite good. Mahon liked beer—within reason. Things took on another glow entirely—a sort of fuzzy aura. Mahon believed in Kirlian photography. Shit, once upon a time not so long before he had actually seen penumbra around objects, and around people too. It had been disturbing at the time, but he had grown accustomed to it. Then the gift / quirk / whatever had vanished.

Bottle after bottle ensued and Mahon was getting quite happy. The dwarf had never actually materialised and Mahon was resigned to plonking down the pingers on the bar top and drinking away steadily. He never saw the money disappear, but it was always gone when he next looked around. The voices had long since dissipated and Mahon felt alone except for the amorphous elfin presence. He wasn't yet hungry and the day seemed intent on remaining at high noon—for the interior of the hotel was swelteringly hot. Why was no one else here, guzzling down frosty bottles of beer as a panacea? Mahon shrugged and poured another glass.

*

Carlos Te Neke sat waiting in the rain. There wasn't much else to do but wait for the others to arrive. Outside it was fair pissing down.

'Fuck it,' he thought, 'the boys better hurry up or I'm off.'

Then he thought more about the money he would get from this deal and the guns it would finance. He closed his eyes and leant back on his broken seat, idly drummin the fingers of one hand on the crusty dashboard.

THREE

When she came into the room—everything changed. It wasn't as dark anymore. She wasn't preternaturally young and she wasn't old either. She wasn't beautiful, yet by no stretch of the imagination was she ugly. She came directly across to Mahon and smiled. No words. She looked around and shrugged. She sensed there was something awry with him—it wasn't just his dishevelled appearance. Christ, he even had a lopsided smirk on his face. She asked him, "Hey, is there anyone around here?"

Mahon missed the question. So Sue—for that was her name—spoke again, a little louder this time, "Is there anybody here, mate?" This time Mahon looked directly at her. He blinked. He stuttered, "Well – er – I'm not too sure actually ... I mean, someone is taking my money and putting beer on the bar ...."

Sue blinked at this reply. It made no sense. "Who?"

"I don't really know ... I've never actually seen anyone."

She walked around to the other side of the bar and poured herself a red wine from the corked carafe sitting on a silver tray next to the spirit bottles. They were smeared in a dusty film and she wiped her fingers vigorously on the towel that lay on the top of a nearby beer crate. It too was quite filthy. 'Yuk', she thought as she returned to where the odd guy was staring at nothing. 'Waste of time ... and why is it so fuckin' quiet in here?'

Sue walked around the edges of the bar. All the tables and chairs were grimy, as if unused. She came across a juke-box, Chrome Majesty, with a playlist that seemed to have stopped several years earlier. She placed a couple of coins in the slot and pushed some buttons. The Doors flooded the quiet spaces of the room. Mahon felt the melody wash over him in warming waves and suddenly he was genuinely happy for the first time in what seemed like eons. Alcohol, space, music—all combined to produce a chill of silent exhilaration.

He smiled to himself.

Sue glanced over at the inanely smirking stranger holding up the counter and smiled herself. He wasn't bad-looking, come to think of it, and her alcoholic intake was moving along nicely, thank you ....

The sex, much later on, when night had invaded the place and the lust to drown whatever demons lay inside them had subsided, was stoned and mellow. Mahon always had marijuana on his person. They drew in tokes inside the saloon. Then they wandered upstairs and found a bed, fully made-up.

The yearning was mutual and they were both satiated. Sue still didn't know the guy's name, nor did it matter, whilst Mahon for his part was lost within himself. Afterwards, they slept copiously, untouched by fears and anxieties—Mahon's first decent slumber of the year. Outside there was no hint anything else was alive—not the squawk of a bird or the tarseal squeals of a bald tyre. Not the cries of a freckled child, nor the rasp of a rusty gate. Nothing. Nada. Zilch.

It was still night when they woke, half-entrapped in each other. They fucked again, semi-dreaming, but this time it was fast and full-on and they didn't know why. It was only after when she rolled up a smoke that they began to talk. "So, what are you doing here ... in this town, anyway?" She asked, drawing in great gulps of tobacco and exhaling out the nearby window. Mahon could only mutter words to the effect that he was passing through, and, later, that he was "bloody hungry."

After rudimentary ablutions, they went in search of food. It was still hot. No one was sequestered in the hotel—nor it seemed in the vicinity. The back-yard was grimy—a plague of dust and weeds with old sheds made from broken and rusty tin. A dead dog lay frying in the sun—its smell reeked of squalor and sordidness. A bevy of rampant flies plied their necrophilic trade over the decaying corpse. Out the front there was nobody in sight, although there seemed to be a high-pitched keening emanating from down the street.

The sun sneaked higher, scaling the sky.

So they rummaged in the kitchen. They strip-searched the fridge. No fresh fare anywhere. Soon Sue had The Doors on again and Mahon found the freezer and the foodstuffs racked inside. There was only one song and Jim Morrison sang about *break on through to the other side*. Mahon knew all the lyrics by heart and sang them, though he had no memory of knowing them. They cooked and ate in peace. Mahon vanquished the entire spread in one mighty swoop, attempting to fill the gnawing gap in his guts. His diet, like his life, lacked consistency. Sometimes he didn't eat for days.

By now, evening had encroached. It remained warm but the pair still had no knowledge of each other's names. It didn't seem to matter. Sue wandered down the street in search of humanity. Mahon started to drink softly, inside. No sounds this time, only the palpitations of his own breath. He did feel—on the whole—a bit better. Not so splintered. His mind had a little more focus. 'Kāore ahau he mōhio,' ran like a mantra through his brain. Mahon often reverted to his original tongue, especially when he was confused or addled, or both. All too often his own language conveyed nuances and meanings that his second-learned, colonially-induced one never could. 'Taurekareka' for example, had connotations of slavery in earlier times in the skinny country, now it had come to be a pejorative: "You fucking taurekareka." 'Upoko mārō' was another phrase he remembered from his childhood oh so many years ago. His mother had always berated him with "ko he tama ki he upoko mārō koe." His mother had always berated him. Had always insisted with her spiteful tongue that he was "abnormal." Which may or may not have been true. Mahon had always been 'difficult.' He could never seem to fit into patterns promulgated by society. He had never voted, remitted tax returns at year's end or filled in a census form. He had a deep abhorrence for systems—regulations and restrictions—and a consequent dislike for anyone who enforced them.

Ironically, Mahon was far from hard-headed now. His brain was reverting to a mélange of what seemed like loose turds, so he grabbed another bottle and began to pour. No payment anymore, for even the goblin had gone. Jim Morrison wouldn't or couldn't shut up.

At one stage later, when he was searching for a bed, he thought he heard someone coughing. What? Another transient there too? Mahon peered around the room. There—recumbent on a rubber lounge settee was a dark figure, his / her white pupil-less eyes peering in anticipation at him.

Mahon stood stock still. He was unsure of what to do, so did nothing. The figure too remained motionless. A stand-off, perhaps? Time passed. Outside the moon glimmered through the slats, benignly.

Finally Mahon broke the stalemate by coughing, "Sorry to – er – interrupt you mate," he stammered, the beer breaking his enunciation into what he felt was an idiotic ramble. "Looking for a bed myself." The dark figure remained quiescent. Only the round white eyes continued to stare relentlessly at Mahon who shuffled uneasily. "Yeah, well ..." Mahon lurched off to go on with his drinking back at the bar. 'Fuck this,' he thought, 'I'm not sleepy anymore.'

Yet Sue found him comatose—snoring, drunk. He muttered some rubbish and fell backwards onto the threadbare carpet. She left him there and went upstairs to sleep.

She had barely anything to report. A couple of closed stores and an old man at the decrepit garage who could only sputter that the town's entire populace had gone to a tangi. Or so she thought—she couldn't remember. Sue had ended up talking to an alpine hitch-hiker, who had given up finding service anywhere, and was preparing to move on down the line. They had shared a racehorse of dope: a thin reefer that the alpine guy had traded earlier for a couple of bars of Nestle.

Sue felt the sweet pangs full her lungs. She was now feeling relaxed, OK. Until she saw Mahon slumped. The marijuana began to wear off and she resolved to escape the place at sunrise. She clambered up the stairs to the same bedroom as before and soon joined Mahon in the Land of Nod.

*

Te Neke had gone into a fitful doze. It was so cold and dank in the leaking vehicle that he had wrapped himself in a ragged army blanket one of his cousins had left in the back seat months before—after a botched job up in the city.

He had given up on his meeting and had given up on the day.

Such was the weather: day had given up unto the sprawling vista of night.

Time passed.

FOUR

Dr Dallas stared out of his window on the fortieth floor of the administrative tower at the drops of spittle portending the inevitable downpour to come. He sighed and sat back in his leather chair reflecting on his morning thus far. It had been a day as mundane as most others, but when one had been in his position for so long life was almost always humdrum and repetitive. Once, Dallas had thought seriously about quitting, but the call of the dollar and his doubts as to what to do with the remainder of his life soon quashed that notion. He did not wish to slide into a benign nonexistence. Besides, would he be allowed to leave?

He fingered his trim beard and glanced at the droplets cascading against the window-panes then picked up the paperback *New New-Age Guide to Psychiatric Postmodernism* and flicked through its copious pages, stumbling here and there over some of the words, some of the names. Even he, as Superintendent Licensing Division, Psychiatric Postmodernism, windy city, skinny country, had some difficulty in keeping up with all of this stuff. He, who himself had typed out a couple of contributions for this very tome, on this very keyboard.

He had almost resigned himself to quietly withstanding his last few years there—without having to get too involved in any cult critique. But the department had been calling out for some sort of rapprochement with Foucault, among others, and Dallas knew he had to make some semblance of effort to appear to know about all this episteme crap. He had no real affection for it, but he knew that he had to keep up the façade of an earnest and erudite professional. He turned over a few pages and farted reflectively while the rain rattled down in an angry chorus outside.

He could of course resign and go home and plant gardenias. But his earlier, somewhat profligate lifestyle, had committed him to making as much money as he could for the next few years. To pay off all those damned credit card bills which seemed to augment exponentially.

Outside, the rain was a torrent. As he reflected on how damnably dull his life was—given that most of his workload had been privatised to the foreign-based monopolies running the prisons, community mental health centres and so on— he was sure that he could make out some letters on the slimy pane outside. From his position— a mere metre or so from the window—Dallas could make out a word or two, if he turned his head a little to the left and kept his eyes sternly focused. The message seemed—and here he could not be certain—to be, FUC YU SONNY

'How odd,' reflected Dallas, as he blinked a couple of times and refocused. There was some doubt in his mind as to what he thought he had just seen. He could no longer quite pick out the letters, in fact, the rainwater had segued into a rivulet now and any legibility was gone.

Dallas sighed again and sat back in the utilitarian leather waiting for the telephone to ring. Something had to happen: someone had to call. Otherwise, what was he doing there? Surely there was more to life than idly drumming one's fingers on a desk, bereft of inspiration, dependant on some other agency's impetus?

And still it poured. Dallas had written the first sentence in his latest article for *Passages*, the dry academic journal that paid so well. It read:

> There can be no doubt that paranoia is pri-
> marily an attention seeking device, designed
> to gain the consideration the paranoid feels
> is his or her due.

He sat back. The water outside was turning the once firm soil into liquid mud and Dallas thought he could make out far below, some goon dressed in a red plastic raincoat, falling arse-over-kite into the squirm; gumboots amuck. But this was only a possible scenario: from so many floors up and in such conditions Dallas could not be certain. Not to mention his eyes were failing him these days and he was inclined to see things that were not there, or were—indeed—something else altogether. He stroked his thinning, greying locks and tried to wring some more from his brain.

> There can be some justification for the para-
> noid's delusional status however. We live in
> an age of sensory over-kill. There no longer
> seems to be a principle via media but several
> cul-de-sacs.

Dallas leant back, proud of this last sentence. He drummed his bony, arthritic fingers on the faded desktop and permitted himself a smile.

> Bifurcation and beyond is now the norma-
> tive state. Blind alleys proliferate, avenues
> turn back upon themselves.

No, he would change that to avenues have sex with themselves.

Just then the telephone did ring.

*

Back out on the endlessly stretching highway, Mahon turned on the radio. The Doors music of the last day — or was it the day before? — had made him want to listen to something else from that era, when life seemed fresher and simpler. He searched the airwaves but could only find static and the pip-pip-pip at the end of the tuner knob's capacity. He rummaged around inside his glovebox. Mahon felt like someone searching for the Holy Grail, the perfect tape, the quintessential sound that would annihilate the chasm. He found nothing.

On the road he saw no other cars, only acres of sheep. Once he saw a horse running feverishly onto the tarseal, its nostrils flaring, froth foaming from its mouth. Wild-eyed, frantic, desperate. Just as it seemed that it would slam into the massive chromed bumpers of the Zephyr it veered off — another out-of-control beast in the wilderness. The two drove on. And on. The sun laughed and bore down on them savagely. The sheep ignored them.

At a distant crossroads Mahon made a decision to turn towards the coast. He felt the need to breathe sea air and roam the dunes. Maybe even to bathe in the waves and wash away some of his burden. He wanted to strip off all semblance of his current self or selves and to resurface a new man, whole and healed. The image kept him driving, driving, driving. The car breathed on up the highway. The road became narrow, curvaceous and hilly.

The Zephyr had to slow more and more: climb, descend, climb, descend. Mahon soon became nauseous with the roundabout motion and stopping the car he vomited furiously out of the window. Splenetic. Virulent. Distasteful in the extreme. He retched and retched his guts out. His inner being came out through his puking mouth and he spewed again. The slime dribbled over his cracked lips. He lay on the side of the road. His body was racked by coughing. It was if every bodily cell was rebelling. Angry. Vengeful. Utu. Mahon's own thin frame wanted revenge on him. This was open warfare between two avowed enemies. Mahon could not lie without pain for every movement was torturous. Even if he tried to wipe his mouth his fingers cried out arthritically and his elbows locked in denial. His knees throbbed and his foot—where he had broken it so many years before in a drugged leap from a train-platform—screamed in agony. Even his hair hurt.

He had often wondered about bodies, and whether there was anything else other than this aging, rather obese shell he walked around in. He would like to transcend this frame but had no idea how to. Not only did it sometimes declare open warfare on him—it often betrayed him at important moments. He thought of the number of times his penis had failed at the moment of penetration and his lady at the time had said "This is not working." The number of times that he had wanted to get somewhere fast and found his body not responding, despite his demands. Mahon's body was 'out of shape.' It farted unduly, ran out of breath, got pissed too easily and felt awful the following day. It fell over and hurt itself too frequently, got all sorts of diseases and often just plain stank. Mahon could not depend on his body: it was untrustworthy.

Mahon lay there a long time. He wondered — between spasms — if this was some sort of karmic interlude. His sins coming home to roost. For Mahon had indubitably committed sins, despite the quaintness of such a notion. He had fornicated. He had taken a vast array of alarming chemicals. He had robbed. Stolen. Beaten his wife. Lied. Ignored his offspring. Exaggerated beyond the bounds of hyperbole. Blasphemed incorrigibly. Lusted after more than one of his neighbour's wives. And daughters. Need we learn more!

His penis groaned. His tongue felt about ten sizes too big for his shrivelled mouth. His eyes throbbed — when he managed to close them he sighted only matt black. He sweated. If he turned to one side or attempted to sit up there was a searing pain in his spine and he collapsed back onto the grass. The Zephyr did nothing. The sheep had gone. Mahon began to make a list of all the bad things that he may have done to deserve this. Shit, the list was way too long and he gave up. It only further depressed him. He began to pray.

*

If it was daytime Te Neke couldn't make it out, it was so damned dark and gloomy. His head throbbed bitterly. Not only because his associates had not arrived as per schedule, but also, because he had found nowhere comfortable to lay his head. His blanket was damp too, from the leaking roof— Te Neke was in a foul mood.

He managed to wind down one of the fucked windows and spat copiously into the streaming rain. He decided to wait a couple of hours and then go back. The meeting was too important to miss. He spat again and bundled himself up as best as he could into his steaming, stinking blanket. A rabbit shot into the dripping fronds of the indigenous bush. The only noise was the rain laughing itself silly against the window outside.

FIVE

Later, when Mahon could finally stand and drive— when his guts crawled back down into the hole from whence they came—he slowly ventured over the remaining kilometres to the beach. It was still only the afternoon, yet he had been on his travail for hours. Time was somehow standing still. The sun did not move in the sky. The road and paddocks were endless. The tractor Mahon had espied from the top of one of the multitudinous hills never shifted from its position. The ubiquitous silence made an unquenchable din inside his ears. They hurt all the more for hearing absolutely nothing—and in their straining to pick up even a whisper, even a semblance of the sea. Mahon came to believe that he was inside a painting, a well-known one, but annoyingly right then, unknown to him. He was waiting for the artist to release him to the waves. Stasis filled Mahon like a torrential flood.

He stroked his Molly laying under the seat. He murmured to her, promising. Something existentially sullen lurked way down in his soul. He felt her firm metal bulk and her hard wooden butt and he smiled to himself, more a grimace than a grin. His insides felt better: not well, not healed—but better.

They were crawling now, a creeping, almost sideways waddle. How appropriate Mahon mused in his Cancerian way. The car had smelt the sea and was clambering its arcane path to the breakers, but progress was tedious, tiresome.

Then they were there.

The last curve suddenly revealed smashing breakers. The whip-crack, salt-sting of air slashed at Mahon's tired eyes. He rubbed them furiously as if he could also wipe away the sickening sway racking his body. No use.

Beside the beach the Zephyr stopped by some boulders. Mahon sat a while, his fatigued brain plodding in an effort to work out what was going on. The events of the past few days, months and years were a blur. His mind was in mothballs.

He farted loudly and copiously. Then belched.

Eventually Mahon wandered on down to the beach, picking his way over driftwood, seaweed and assorted rubbish. Negotiating the slalom of logs, rocks and holes in the ground. Clambering over sleek drenched stone: down, down, down, to the very wave-front itself. The beach was huge, pervasive—infinite. Above, a few gulls screeched maniacally, and, faintly in the distance over the murmur of the waves, Mahon could hear the thud thud thud of some machinery, perhaps farm equipment, perhaps not. By the water was a pile of papers: sea-drenched and sodden.

One or two pages had worked their way loose from the group and were lashing against Mahon's bare feet. A double-spread wound its way around his calves and as he stooped in an effort to swat it away he noticed a headline 'EUROPEAN TEAM LIKELY TO SUFFER AT HANDS OF ...' was all he could decipher. Underneath were a couple of pictures of football players with captions in incomprehensible type. Then there was a list of names, possibly the European team, Baudrillard, Lyotard, Deleuze, Guattari, Foucault, Barthes, Derrida and Lacan were the forward pack. It seemed Merleau-Ponty was captain and some of the other backs—it appeared—were Sartre, Camus, Marcel, Dumery, de Chardin, Comte, Rousseau, Levinas and Bourdieu. Later—long after Mahon had thrown away the deconstructed paper—he wondered why there were so many players in the backline, but this synapse soon departed as he trudged on.

He felt much better—earlier he couldn't have felt much worse. The air was clear and invigorating. He paused once or twice to inhale and felt the acerbic atmosphere revitalize his lungs. The zephyr blowing from a-far was cathartic and purgative. It was if he were rebuilding his inner soul. Mahon's depression began to lift but this time without the influx of alcohol. The shadows in his head faded the further he strode. Up above, the sun gnawed at him. He stripped to the waist and carted his clothing like a flag of surrender above his head in an effort to make shade. It was hellish hot. He was walking slowly now, the sand cooler closer to the water. His footprints were impressed upon this damp sand and he looked back at their pattern. He pulled up his jeans haphazardly and began to paddle in the water. It was colder than he had anticipated, but after the first stings, he enjoyed the sensation of the scurries of water embalming his feet. 'Christ,' he thought, 'my feet need a bloody good clean.'

He stripped completely and ran headlong into the surf letting the water rage all over him. He dived under the cascades feeling the salt drive up his nose, burn in his throat, eat into his eyes. He dived under again. He swam a few half-hearted strokes and then stood up. Without his shades he was myopic and could see nothing beyond a hazy string of sand and the multicoloured jumble that was his clothes.

He played around for some time in the ocean like

a school-kid just released on the first day of holidays. Finally he stumbled up the beach and lay dripping near his clothes. The combined heat of sun and sand soon dried him off completely. He could feel his body burning up and a delicious warmth spreading through his aging joints, deep into every pore of his skin. He was tremendously tired, and, dressing spasmodically, he climbed his way up the dunes.

Mahon slept fitfully under a tree and woke to the sound of chanting. Someone had been observing him. Just a few metres away was the easy figure of an old man. He kaumātua, nē rā. He was white-headed and white-bearded, his face burnt a deep brown and he clasped a stick of driftwood with which he was shovelling great mounds of dry sand into a heap. He was chanting in his own tongue seemingly oblivious to the gaunt man of his own race who slumbered beneath the tree.

Mahon watched for a while before he crouched, rubbing his eyes. The man had facial tattoos. His chant was rhythmic, addictive, and Mahon felt himself drawn into its web. He let the word-sounds sweep over him assuaging his inner sanctum. The chant crept into his crevasses, pervaded his pores.

Then it stopped and Mahon felt the man's eyes on him. Rather, his eye, for Mahon saw that the old man had one stray eye which never focused on much at all, but looked outwards, as if to something else entirely.

The man spoke quietly to the barefoot stranger.

"You seem to have lost your way, son." He was not

patronizing. More, stating the obvious. He began to mutter again, and, after a while Mahon could pick up the words of a prayer that he had learnt many years ago. Karakia. As the man drew towards the culmination Mahon himself muttered "Āmine" in assent. He realized that he was being prayed for—prayed on, prayed about. Again, words did not seem to mount up to what he meant—his language, the signifier, could not find the signified. There was a huge gap between what was written, spoken and read, and that which he wanted to describe. Sometimes he felt the need to invent new words to recapture old worlds, sometimes indeed he felt that the environs he dwelt in were obscenely alien to how others depicted them. That he lived in another dimension entirely.

The old man desisted in his travail and they sat together, scanning seaward. Birds swooped above them and in the background was the distant— thud thud thud—vanishing and returning with the breeze. Suddenly the man stood up and strode down toward the waves. He was peering seaward intently. Mahon had no idea what he was doing or what—if anything—the deep hole was for. The older one continued to gaze. His whole posture intent: taut and upright. His gaze fixed on some secretive centre point.

He remained that way for some time as Mahon watched him, fascinated. The man was like a dog waiting for its prey: tail poised, paws firm, head erect.

Neither spoke for sometime until Mahon—sensing a lull in the other's surveillance—asked what his name was. "Tamati, son," was the gruff reply.

"I sometimes come here to find things. To search the sands. Best place. Tapu land though. No good for a young fellow like you. Mōhio koe taku kupu e hoa?"

Mahon nodded—he believed that he did comprehend Tamati, although he didn't. For Tamati's words had deeper nuances than Mahon was capable of gleaning.

The old man had some sort of mana, some strong presence. He almost seemed part of the landscape, rooted to the dunes. Tamati fetched a pouch from his pockets and began to roll a cigarette, he lit up and drew the sweet tobacco in, in deep gusts.

Later they made a fire right there on the shore, stacking scattered timbers and flotsam into a pyre that gave off even more heat than the great yellow beast in the sky. Tamati crouched and drew food from deep in his finely-woven kete, then set about boiling a billy filled with water from one of the streams that warbled to the sea. Tamati existed on this beach when he wasn't at hui. Mahon had yet to view the old man's hut, hidden under a rock face, shaded from both salt spray and sun.

They drank down the biting brew, sharing the one chipped enamel mug Tamati fished out of his bag. Mahon admired the finely carved manaia hanging from the neck of the kaumātua and found himself fondling the more basic design of his own one.

Tamati seemed at peace with himself. His many wrinkles the earned signs of age.

Mahon pondered if he could ever be as settled as the old man so evidently seemed to be. He ran his fingers once again through his greying locks and recalled an article, 'Tangential Man', he had had published many years before when he was casting himself in the role of philosopher.

But Mahon's mind was called on by Tamati asking him if he was hungry and announcing that anyway, he was, and that it was time for a "kai eh boy."

The fire raged on.

Tamati sloped off somewhere while Mahon went for a piss and when he had put his dribbling dick away and re-zipped his sandy jeans, Tamati was already back, frying up eggs and lamb chops.

"Nicked these yesterday, man. Saw a stray lamb and sliced its bloody neck. Fresh man, fresh." Tamati literally lived off the land. The watercress he was boiling in the same battered billy was ripped from the stream-banks further inland whilst the eggs had "fallen off the back of a truck."

"No bread, sorry mate ... but this'll do, eh?"

Mahon was about to wolf down the kai when Tamati began the blessing. Mahon felt himself blush. Fuck, he had forgotten another karakia.

E Ihowa,
Whakapaingia ēnei kai
He oranga mō ō mātou tinana
Whāngaia hoki ō mātou wairua

Ki te taro ō te ora
Ko Ihu Karaiti tō mātou Ariki
Ake, ake, ake
Āmine

They ate quite slowly, given their respective hungers. Mahon was tired. Soul-tired. That, combined with the fact that he had been on the run from himself for so long, had slept so little in ages, and that he had eaten something a bit more substantial than his usual fare, whacked him into an instant, heavy slumber.

Later Tamati showed him his hut. It was still bright and burning outside but Mahon sleep-walked with the old man and soon lay dormant in his abode, flat as he could be on the soft springy plantation that Tamati had fashioned there as his mattress. Mahon's feet stuck out from under the greatcoat the old man must have thrown over him: he was oblivious to the act, snoring ad infinitum.

Tamati began another low chant in his peoples' tongue, a rhythmic repetition using many of the same sounds as before, an incantation that went on and on. He scarcely paused for breath. Stripped to the waist he toiled away in the heat, digging what seemed like a trench to the other side of the world. He had gathered a few boulders—seared with age and what looked like burning—into a small mountain near this pit. He was making, perhaps, some sort of oven. That, or a grave.

Mahon slept on.

*

He heard the roars of the bikes as they rummaged the thin coastal roads well before he saw them or the other car. From their dull but distant thrum thrum thrumming he figured they must be around the swamp somewhere. They'd be a while yet.

Te Neke opened the door and peered out. The incessant deluge had abated but it was still wet out there. Not wet enough to prevent the hui, but wet enough to piss you off. He trod across the clay field to a large old tree and tried to shelter from the drip-feed of drops splashing onto his unkempt mop of hair. He thrust his left hand into his leathers and grasped the weapon. Just in case.

A shrill magpie flew swiftly past him from the bush, bent on some unknown mission.

It remained waiting time. He had no choice.

SIX

When Mahon woke he could still hear the dull thud thud thud coming from somewhere. He grappled with his eyes and sat up in the shade. It was hot.

The old man was nowhere in sight. Mahon circumnavigated the ashes of the fire from the night before, looked up and down the expanse of sand and shrugged his shoulders.

People had a bad habit of disappearing—came into his life fleetingly and then just vanished. Where had Sue gone? He thought for the first time.

He trudged on down the beach as the cackling hyena heat above him roared.

Tamati's hole was gargantuan. The place was a tomb. Or a shrine. No sign of the man though. Yet, what was that way down there by what seemed like a river cascading to the waves? A fisherman, perhaps, or maybe two boys standing one on the other, for the figure was curiously double-jointed. He rubbed his eyes, as if in so doing he would conjure 'reality' out of his blurry sight. Join the dots in the paint-by-numbers set that we call vision.

*

The bloody sheep was well and truly mired in the mud of the perennial wallow of that section of the farm. McWilliams didn't have the money to fully drain the area, besides which, he had plenty of other more productive pasture. The more it struggled the more the beast kept sinking lower into the bog. McWilliams knew from prior experience that it would soon surrender. That's when he would rope it and drag it. Couldn't afford to lose anymore stock. Not now his situation had altered so much.

He whistled to his dogs to come back from chasing a couple of other strays. They would wait a bit before tackling this stupid one.

McWilliams sighed and wiped the beads of sweat from his forehead with an old smelly cloth. He would have to go back to the homestead and fix up some food for the kids—they'd be back from school soon. He thought he heard the distant tat-tat-tat of the school bus horn. Another bloody chore he had been saddled with since Kate had gone bloody dopey and left him. Well, sort of left him—she was supposed to be coming back soon with their daughter. No telling how long she would stay this time.

The sheep baaaed forlornly.

McWilliams found himself thinking about why Kate had joined that sect. 'More like a bloody coven,' he grimaced to himself. That Faye Swine had a hell of a lot to answer for. And who was that other one? Bobby somebody or other? Kate had gone distant and started proselytizing about her 'rights and dominions'. She used to disappear up to the city for meetings. Just left the kids there and went. The farm work had suffered and so had their bank balance. Not to mention their relationship.

McWilliams spat into the turf as one of his dogs pissed on a bedraggled, moss-covered fence post. No, he was stuck here too—as much as the sheep.

He thought of his old war buddy, Mahon, and wondered what he would be up to now. Hadn't heard from him for a long time. He often used to come to their spread back in the good old days when the family was bound and bright: even brought his kids a couple of times. Still, McWilliams mused, I wouldn't want to be Mahon. No security. Could end up anywhere. Strange guy. Good soldier, but couldn't be trusted—maybe because he had been conscripted and wasn't too keen on even being there. Could never be certain what he was doing at any given time, which was no good when out on patrol in that damned tropical bush, infested by enemies who merged with the plants. Sometimes Mahon's premonition of danger would save their arses: at other times he was listless, lethargic, uninspired. Erratic. Shit, what about that time they went deer hunting way up on the hill on the back side of the farm and Mahon had just vanished. Still, he had come back with a six pointer ... his chain of recall was broken by the silence of the sheep. It lay there, eyes vacant, mouth twitching noiselessly, staring at him while the dogs waited, their tongues lolling, anticipating his command.

As he bent to tie the rope securely, digging huge piles of mud away from the animal's sunken front legs with his swarthy hands, he also remembered that there was a meeting at the marae that night. Protest meeting about the proposed new military base to be built nearby — on tapu land. He would have to go to that if only to voice his antagonism.

He respected the grievance. Shit, he was as much an Indigenous around here as anyone, even if he wasn't racially. Fifth generation. His family had farmed here for umpteen years. He was part of the furniture he reckoned — and so did most of the locals as far as he knew. He reckoned old Bunny would be along tonight, ironically all fired up about those 'bloody whitemen!'

What would he do with the boys that evening? Had to come with him he guessed. Pity Kate wasn't around though.

He spat again and wrenched the recumbent mutton free. Swatted away a fly or two from his neck, wincing as he felt the sunburn, and strode over to the tractor waiting patiently on the rise.

*

Mahon started to come to his senses and he saw now that what he had mistakenly thought was a fishing pole, or a hockey stick, or some such, was merely a tree bereft of twigs. He began to consider, on closer appraisal, that what seemed to be a misshapen human body was no more than the bloated carcass of a large fish, beached on the shore ahead. He strode on more confident by the minute, as his brain began to quicken.

Thud thud thud echoed sonorously. Mahon still could not work out from where the rhythm came, but it seemed to be growing louder and louder. He reached the dead fish reclining under the dead tree, and, finding the odour sacrilegious to his nostrils, sharply veered up and away from the waves and towards the hypnotic pulse. The sound seemed to be inseparable from the dirt track he was striding along, among the rusted soft-drink cans and coconut husks. Thud thud thud. Thud thud thud. What could it mean?

A corroded factory appeared, in the middle of nowhere, a few metres off the beach. A tall hulk of levels and wheels going around and around; the thud thud thud seemed to emanate from the very top and reverberate all the way through to the base rock beneath the structure. It hissed and squeaked and coughed and belched in perpetual motion. Mahon could see no earthly reason whatsoever for the monstrosity; it did not seem to produce anything. No one seemed to be operating it. Nothing seemed to generate its momentum and nothing was spewing from its many layers of pipage. Mahon scratched his scalp and looked here, there and everywhere.

High up, he spotted someone sweating away, wielding what seemed to be a giant crescent spanner on one of the whirring cogs. On closer peering, Mahon saw the man was wearing grimy overalls, had a neckerchief throttled around his throat and was shirtless and sweating. Large spots of some sort of filthy fluid were spewing down toward Mahon. The man was working manically. He began to hammer the living shit out of one of the pipes so savagely that rust flakes showered from the platform. Meanwhile the thud thud thud continued deep down in the innards of the bedrock itself.

Mahon was—strangely for one so alienated from ordinary discourse—motivated to call out to the high figure. "Hello," he yelled more than once, then, louder and louder each time. "Hello, hello, hello."

No response. Mahon yelled once more—as loud as could be bothered to. "Hello, you fucking idiot," he shouted, "what the fuck are you doing up there?" Mahon didn't expect a response to this, which is why he was so laissez-faire with his comments, but he soon heard a faint "Keeping things going, mate," float down with the rust flakes and the grimy oil fluid. Mahon shook his head in bewilderment.

"When are you coming down, mate?" He implored the distant man.

No reply again, and it took a while for it to dawn on Mahon's quasi-active mental apparatus that the guy up above was never going to 'come on down'. When it did Mahon walked away, while the thud thud thud continued.

Suddenly he felt the need to find his own car and start again on his voyage to God only knew where.

Mahon thought back to his early years—as the Zephyr prowled down the coast road, sweeping around the swathe of foothills and their nauseating curves. His was a dysfunctional family through and through. An alcoholic father who became more alcoholic as time jaundiced, who searched for the cooking sherry if regular 'plonk' ran out. A snobbish mother—a bastard in her own right—who disowned her Indigenous past and tried to dismiss it by way of absurd upward social climbing, which pushed her farmer-boy husband further into diurnal drunkenness. His parents had nothing in common whatsoever and only Mahon, the first born, another little bastard, served to rationalize their domestic arrangements. Other siblings arrived later, but by that time there was no communication between Mater and Pater except a fist in the face and the concomitant sunglasses the next day.

Mahon's father died ignored, and in agonizing pain, at the young age of 49. Couldn't make 50. Lying cancer-ridden, half his former size, in a side bedroom. His wife out at work. Back then, when his ESP functions were flying high, Mahon picked up the man's death vibrations and raced to a telephone to confirm with a helpful neighbour. He shot down to Dirty City in a few hours flat, to be at his father's bedside before he went sideways into the big sleep. Mahon's final recollections of his Dad were the shit stains from his last living effort and his mother's off-hand shrug, "At least he was happy," which was so patently stupid that Mahon could never forget the words. What the fuck was the meaning of his father's life? It seemed a complete waste of time. Mahon prayed that some bloodline fault would not carry him down the same hasty de/incline.

He had once—when very young—believed that all Gods, religions, drugs, mantras and doc-trines were absurd—we were all going to die any-way. Some more silently than others, some at their own hands, some tomorrow. Some in car smashes, some when they choked to death on their din-ner. And all the shit rolling around in their heads would signify sweet fuck-all. All the potty train-ing, peer-group pressure, sibling rivalry. Except, as his life lengthened, Mahon also sensed—indeed had seen—vistas of something more shock-ingly profound, despite and beyond his rationalisa-tions. It was just that they had escaped him of late. Only jaded snapshots of them lingered.

Mahon didn't want sympathy or even therapy.

His tape deck appeared to have wound itself to death so he went to the radio. There was music there, but it was so far, far away that Mahon could not make out either the tune or the lyrics. Static filled the radio's every band when Mahon attempted to switch stations. People were there, and they were talking, but they were not talking to Mahon. It was if a thin veil was stretching between his ears and those manipulating the radio waves. He switched off the device and peered ahead.

Time for Jimmi.

*

The first bike lurched over the low rise and into view. Hemi—for Te Neke recognised his massive beard protruding under the black crash helmet he always wore—clambered off the chopper and stretched his legs, cursing. He eyed Te Neke slotted against the tree trunk and cracked into a broken-toothed smile.

"Kia ora bro." He waited until Te Neke trudged over to him and gave him the greeting—hand formed into fist.

"Fucking took your time, man," groaned Te Neke, "where's the other bastards?" He needn't have spoken, for two big old bikes just then chugged into view, followed by a worn out Chrysler replete with dual aerials, chrome, and fat tyres on the back. It sounded as if it was suffering a long, lingering death.

There were seven of them, counting Matipo's wahine beautifying the back of his Harley. Fat Man stayed in the back of the car, watching. The others sloped over to the two cousins—stretching, yawning, sizing him up. Te Neke didn't know these fellows so good. No salutes, no chatter. Just sidelong glances. One of them removed his gloves.

"Got the stuff, man?" Enquired Sucker, sweeping off his shades and squinting at Te Neke. Sucker always got down to business straight away.

"Got the dough, bro?" Was all Te Neke could muster. He was all too aware that the others had spread around the back of him—smoking, pissing, watching. Hemi stood nearby, feigning deafness.

"Sure, man. No worries. You get it when we see the goods."

Te Neke went over to the Valiant and creaked open the only rear door that worked. Reaching in he pulled out a small plastic bag then loped back over to Sucker who had taken off his jacket in the hot sun.

Te Neke rolled a couple of very large spliffs and lit them separately, passing them to the gathering. One to the right, one to the left. Fat Man stayed where he was. Te Neke didn't partake.

They drew the fumes in deeply, then exhaled—a couple of them coughing at the sheer strength of Te Neke's crop. It was getting hotter all the time. Carlos rolled up his black jersey sleeves.

After some time Sucker beamed and scratched his prison-inked face. "Fucking hell man, this is good shit all right. We'll take as much as you can get."

The others rested in a variety of poses, some sitting back on bikes, some squatting on the clay. Matipo's woman was combing her long hair under the trees. A couple were laughing about something by the bridge. These guys were almost caricatures of themselves. Walking clichés.

Carlos smiled inwardly but revealed nothing. "I've got it, but not here ... let's go back into town and celebrate the deal. I need a beer or two after waiting for you bastards out here for so long. I can get the rest there, where I've stashed it ..." he lied. He didn't want the boys to know exactly where he kept his crop, let alone grew it. Hadn't been his idea to meet way the fuck out here. Besides which, he needed more time to think. He didn't trust most of these fellows. Weren't his usual running crew. Only Hemi was whanaunga. 'Not my bloody iwi,' he thought.

"Sounds good to me," pointed out Hemi, "I need a beer too."

"And a scrap," added Matipo, grinning.

They formed a scrappy procession out on the disjointed, curving track, back to the main highway and thence to 'town', such as it was. It was quite a few kilometres away and still Te Neke couldn't quite work out why the meeting had been out here, something to do with 'narcs' and 'dobbers' according to Hemi, who first put him onto these guys. Why then had Sucker agreed so readily to go back? Some things made no sense.

Te Neke drove on, ruminating. He felt he was

enmeshed in a Lee Tamahori movie. Shit, next thing would be a bloody scrap in some pub! He resolved to stay straight.

SEVEN

Mahon braked as soon as he saw the guy on the side of the road. The screeches drew him and the Zephyr up about 150 metres further along the lane, but so what. The guy—if he really wanted a lift—would catch up. Mahon nearly always braked for figures on the side of the road, except likely arseholes, then he sped up.

He waited while the figure ran towards the Zephyr, turning Hendrix, as he zoomed everything dead with some insane riff, lower.

"Kia ora e hoa," said Mahon, his surprising act snapping him out of his reminiscence. "Jump in." He nodded to the seat space beside him. "Where ya headed, mate?" He continued, almost loquacious by his recent standards. The guy said nothing. Lugubrious, taciturn, say what you will, his new passenger with hollow cheeks, haunted eyes and hacking cough was not exactly talkative. Mahon, by comparison, was logorrhoea personified.

Later, he learnt that the cadaverous chap was called Franz, and he was touring the skinny country, had a finite budget and was a writer back in his home land—some strange sounding, middle-European nexus with a gloomy heritage. Another knight of the road, not smitten by domesticity, mortgages and nappies. A paid-up member of the thin league of road people. It transpired that Franz was lost, had taken some oblique turning somewhere and had wandered without a sense of direction until some large tank-like machine had stopped by the side of the road and picked him up. He was glad of that and tried to convey this to the bleary-eyed driver—but the guy seemed like a space cadet. Franz coughed and spat out the window. Mahon couldn't speak Franz's language and had enough trouble articulating his own. Franz was unwilling/unable to transliterate anything cogent for most of their journey on the spartan back roads of the skinny country. It was a transit doomed to silence and a few spasmodic grunts and groans. Franz seemed withdrawn into himself completely: his eyes shrunken into their wide staring sockets. He looked like a refugee, or one of those TB victims that Mahon had seen in photos. Or something out of a concentration camp. Mahon flickeringly recalled that such places were worldwide phenomena now.

The sun blared down caustically, as if in vengeance.

At a crossroads further down the line was a ramshackle hotel-come-restaurant surrounded by buildings, masquerading as a town. Mahon needed a drink—and, increasingly, to talk to someone.

Inside the bar were a few sturdy patrons, regulars, by the look of their 'who-gives-a-fuck' attitude towards dress. One big guy with a beard was sculling schooners of draught beer whilst another smaller bearded guy in a swandri was sinking balls on the faded pool table. The barman was reading a newspaper. He took off his reading glasses as the odd couple wandered in—a long-haired, greying guy and a remarkably skinny, frail looking other, with wildly vacant eyes. This latter one had a nose which was way too big for his face.

Mahon ordered two beers, as Franz could have been from another planet as far as any dialogue was concerned. Still, he could drink beer no problems. He was twice as fast as Mahon and showed no ill-effects. Mahon was reminded of a favourite saying from one of his old war cronies, 'Busier than a one-legged man at a bum-kicking competition.' Franz drank as if death was chasing him.

The bearded two-some were pig hunters from 'up the valley,' having a lull time before they went back up boots 'n' all. They shared a couple of games of pool, although Franz was useless—and Mahon had thought that he was bad. The barkeeper just read his paper, even though Mahon had glanced at the top of the column and noticed that it was over a week old. He also believed, but could not prove it, dear reader, that the man's glasses had no lenses in them.

Slowly more and more oddball chaps sauntered in.

Barry and Larry were okay, thought Mahon. Not too bright, but hey, so what? Who needed intelligence to play pool, drink draught beer and sometimes shoot porky pigs?

"Where you from, mate?" Was Barry's only statement all afternoon. Larry gossiped only a little more — about horses and the local market — so that their communication came more in the form of gestures, grunts and grimaces. The stock talk was quite literally that. Talk about ewes and lambs, heifers and pig dogs, geldings and porkers. An exchange of the eccentric. A lexicon of the lost.

Deep into the day Franz wandered off never to be seen again. His gnome-like frame was last sighted by Mahon slumped, like a used dish-rag, over the worn-out bar. His jug had been empty and Franz was too. Even his eyes had vacated the premises. Mahon didn't care. Wasn't his problem. He had enough of his own. Barry and Larry had thrashed them at pool and didn't seem interested in any more such one-sided sessions. The barman had gone and a clone had arrived to take his place. Or maybe it was his stunt double, dressed in a different shirt. Some sort of doppelganger. Mahon wandered erratically toward the jukebox and started more sounds from the psychedelic era: a generation his mind had stalled in.

I see a red door and I want to paint it black

No colours anymore when your whole world is black ...

Later in the afternoon Mahon shuffled out into the carpark. The vehicles out there were old, weather-beaten jobs — rather like his own piebald car — a couple of obligatory dice hanging, like a caricature, in the front windows. Large mismatched tyres on some wheels. A couple of dogs were sunning themselves outside the entrance to the bar. Mahon pissed all over the weeds by the rusty corrugated iron palisade and then went back inside.

Someone else was playing pool now and someone had started up the jukebox. It sounded like Elvis Presley of all people. Some inane song that wasn't even a parody, though it sounded like one. Elvis, or whoever, droned on and the pool balls pinged off the corners of the table. Cigarette smoke was a thick pall in the air. Franz may as well have been dead. Maybe he was. That would explain his quietness. Mahon drank on.

This bar was similar to thousands of others throughout the skinny country. They all came out of the same book, drawn by the same artist, pages of them one after the other: pool tables, flat beer, Brylcreem, cigarette clouds, meat pies, fights to break the monotony, more flat beer. If there was any cogent pattern in this country it was in these bars. The juke box always seemed to play the same three songs. Christ, thought Mahon, even the people all looked the same: swandris, work boots, tattoos, singlets, ripped check-shirts, stubbled chins, fag-ends spewing out their lips, pool cues looming like grotesque appendages from their sides. At one stage he thought he saw a group of gang members in the gloom, but he wasn't certain.

Elvis sang on. The smoke was fog. The pool-men had become more manic. Mahon drank solidly. He then had another of his brain glitches when a mental gear seemed to slip. He became confused.

Another bloody deja-vu flicker: he had been in this scene elsewhere. Too many times. It was somehow becoming hotter as well. Mahon had become quite intoxicated—with the mellowness that goes with that state. Not caring, not concerned about what comes next. Incredibly randy. He sighed as he lifted his gaze and glanced around the walls. The photographs of ancient football teams lined them along with a long-deceased race horse or two. Old calendars, beer stains and some banal/anal graffiti. The cigarette smoke was so dense that Mahon's eyes began to water.

When the fight started Mahon had just come back inside after another Herculean urination and was minding his own business in the corner, dully sipping an ale. He was unprepared for the incredible blow from behind that crashed him to his knees and smashed his head on the table, bringing up stars and planets that orbited his closed eyes. 'Jesus,' his stupefied brain asked, 'what the fuck goes on?' Jesus preferred to be left out of the equation.

Already one or two other bodies were floundering over him, obviously as bewildered as himself. Bottles were flying all over the place, as were humans, and the previously guttural tones had become yells and screams and violent oaths. Mahon knew that he had to get out of there and get out of there fast, so he started crawling towards the door. He wasn't the only one. His knees were sodden from what could have been beer or blood or piss—who knew in this muddle? And his head hurt. The fight raged on and on. The pool table must have been up-ended because multi-coloured balls went rolling before Mahon's dizzy vision, 11, 7, 9.

Outside, it had become night and the relative coolness of the air sobered Mahon a little. As he rose from his crawl into a shaky stoop he could see a few others like himself standing around—lighting up, throwing up, blinking and cursing.

"What's going on?" Asked a young lady who had appeared beside him. She seemed shaken.

"Who knows?"

"I'm glad I'm not still inside."

"Makes two of us. Bit quick that one. First thing I knew I was on the floor."

"You're bleeding – no – over that eye," and so Mahon was. Blood was pumping out of a gash and soaking into the carpark grime. Mahon had felt nothing, had not even sensed that he was bleeding so profusely.

"Shit."

"I've got some towels in the car. Hang on a minute."

She was back very quickly, dabbing her towels on the wound, stemming the torrent. Mahon muttered a silent thanks. 'Fuck it,' he thought. Her name was Karin and she was beautiful. Mahon realized this when the blood flow was staunched and he was able to see more clearly. The reason he found out her name was that her car number plates had 'Karin 1' etched on them. So he put two and two together. 2 + 2 = 4. Ask Mr Heisenberg.

Some prone bodies still littered the carpark and somewhere someone was going berserk on bottle-smashing. No doubt the police—wherever they came from in such a remote place—had been called in by now.

Mahon sighed and felt sobriety overwhelm him. He noticed Karin was looking with grave concern into his eyes which felt as if they were roller-coasting all over his face. She led him to sit down on the front seat of her petite car parked in the corner away from the melee. He felt his penis stiffen as she inspected his wound.

"You were a little lost out there you know?" Said Karin.

"Yeah, I – er – don't remember much about it. I guess I was a bit dazed." Mahon began to recall that he had been talking to this young lady inside. For quite some time too. If only he could remember what about. His brain was still in semi-shutdown mode. When they kissed Mahon felt straight away that he was in love. Love was a strange thing, reflected Mahon. It was so intangible, so ephemeral, so weird that it could have been an LSD tab. Mahon had seen grown adults metamorphose most peculiarly from their new-found, amorous cocoon. Men had ceased drinking, whoring, swearing—had gone home at reasonable hours, washed dishes, swept floors and even mowed the lawns. Worse still, they weren't even their lawns.

Karin placed Roxy Music into her tiny car's tape deck as they stole out onto the main road. *Love is the drug* insidiously wound itself around their entwined bodies.

Their lovemaking—back at Karin's battered old flat out in the farmlands—was bliss: honeyed and nightlong.

"That was good," said Karin as she lit up a joint and drew on it gently. "That was fine."

"Yeah," murmured Mahon, his brain gyrating on the sheer pleasure. Some creature deep inside his brain was licking itself contentedly, smugly.

*

Zita didn't say anything to Matipo after the hui. She was sick to fucking death of him and his stupid hoha ways. She sulked on the back of the bike as they sped round the bends and wolfed down the grades into 'town'.

She stayed silent in the pub too. Each time he tried to talk to her or raise a smile on her bruised lips she just pouted more, accentuating the deep moko emblazoned on her chin. Her eyes told him to leave her the fuck alone, so he did, and proceeded to get drunker and angrier.

Zita knew who would throw the first punch, 'Fuck this,' she thought, 'I'm outta here.' She had been thinking of getting out of the whole gang scene for a while now, anyway.

She stumbled shakily over to the carpark door, then skulked for a while by the corrugated iron wall, clicking through her options.

EIGHT

Mahon woke well into the next morning, knowing he had to get back out on the road. He was restless, worried he might have to make commitments. Act responsibly. Mow lawns. Karin was still sound asleep. He crept out of her king-sized bed as quietly as he could.

Out in the muggy day he rubbed his head, then thought 'Where is the car?' Still in that hotel park, he hoped. He shrugged, then set off on foot for the few kilometres slog into the village. Maybe somebody would give him a ride. He stuck out his thumb in imitation of Franz.

A lazy tractor stopped to pick him up. Mahon climbed onto the back tray so didn't speak to the hooded driver. He doubted the driver spoke a mutual lingo anyway, for he looked distinctly foreign. Finally, Mahon strolled down the few backstreets towards where he thought the hotel was. It couldn't be far away — the village wasn't big enough. It was one of those places where you could see the end of it when you hit the beginning. Rounding a corner, bypassing some kids booting a fucked-looking football, he saw the hotel and also his car — from this distance it seemed to have all of its tyres. It was still there anyway — that in itself was amazing.

When he reached it, after jumping over a few fences and running awkwardly through someone's backyard, he made a rudimentary inspection of the previously scratched paintwork, unlocked the door and jumped in. He started it up, first time, and shot out of the car park, revving a bit for effect, zooming off towards wherever. He smiled as he inspected his face in the mirror, noticing the dark anaemic circles etched under his eyes. The car performed effortlessly as if replenished after its slumber. Hendrix did too, even though his guitar was more fuzz than usual due to the blitzed heads on the Zephyr's tape deck. That Karin would have woken by now, and been more than a little pissed off at his absence, made no in-roads into Mahon's conscience.

*

Up in Dirty Inner-City, Bobby Riley was reading *The Gay Express*. An article by Cindy Nightspoiler was confirming Bobby's beliefs about suburban husbands: lazy, misogynist blowhards who subjugated all women—all days—always. Bobby could feel her anger rising. Choler was never very far from the surface in Bobby Riley and it didn't take much to set her into anti-male tirades, especially to Lucy her live-in lover—who should have been home by now—where was she anyway? Bobby put down the broadsheet and drummed her fingers on the formica table. Lucy had said she was just going round to Holly's to borrow some gabardine for the party tomorrow night. Bobby liked to keep tabs on her partner: she was self-admittedly territorial as far as that sort of thing went. 'I'll give her another half an hour and then I'll ring up Holly,' she thought, as she opened a bottle of cheap red wine and poured herself a peanut-butter glass full. On the radio a vixen sang something about losing her man, so Bobby abruptly snapped it off and sung to herself.

She was still daydreaming about her day in the council-depot office when Lucy lurched in, a little the worse for wear. Bobby didn't want an out-an-out confrontation, but she wanted Lucy to know that she—Lucy—should have been more considerate of her—Bobby. It was two hours after she said she would be home after all. And besides which, Bobby didn't really trust Holly's wandering eyes. Even though Holly was married. That didn't mean a bloody thing. Look at Bobby, she used to be married too—to a wimp who couldn't fuck her good. Even back then she had preferred women lovers. A pity she hadn't seduced more young girls back when she was a bit less moralistic. With her recent campaigning and her high-level profile in the council she couldn't afford too much sex-on-the-side with near juveniles. And, to be honest, her hormones had been letting her down lately.

"You said you'd be home ages ago Lucy, where the hell were you?"

"Jesus, Bob, I'm here now, what's the problem?"

"I was getting worried ... and besides, I wanted to put on dinner and didn't know what you wanted." (This last part was an out-and-out lie as Bobby shirked cooking at the best of times.)

"Fuck Bob, you're a control freak."

"What were you doing all that time over at her place? You said you were only going for material."

"Owway, we got to talking about this and that and you know, she likes a wine, so I said yes and we had one or two. What's the problem? You're not my fuckin' mother—that's who I tried to get away from, remember!"

Bobby Riley shut up, and after a bit began to peel potatoes in an effort to back up her earlier words. She cooked as best as she could, and later all seemed forgiven when Lucy kissed her on the nape of the neck and stroked her bum in just the place that Bobby liked it, which made her hornier than hell. "Later, darling, later," was all she could muster, because it was getting bloody hard to braise the meat whilst her twat was melting. After dinner they made love and uttered endearments about never loving anyone else or ever going to in the future, and all that stuff lovers are inclined to say, even believe, in those situations. Shit, anything seems the world / the word when you are so aroused.

Next morning, early, Bobby was up and out in the kitchen downing coffee after coffee and chain-smoking 'rollie' cigarettes. She was still anxious about something, but couldn't quite pinpoint what it was—a sort of free-floating intuition that something bad was going to happen: a vague sense of foreboding that she had better be prepared for the worse. For some reason Bobby began to think about her old friend Fay Swine who had died a couple of years back after suffering a massive stroke which had so incapacitated her that she could only lie in a room dribbling, unable to open her eyes. 'Fuck that,' mused Bobby. 'No way, no how.'

Bobby recalled the day that they had laid Faye to rest—all the old gang were there, from Betty Mae Brown who still hadn't quite opened the closet door, to the staunch bitches from the Fuck-you Lesbian League. They had given Faye one hell of a send-off that afternoon. Wine and tears had flowed, and they had told tales tall and true about Faye's exploits: like the time she had set fire to her husband when he came home pissed one time too many and retched all over the kitchen. Faye had been a legend in the women's liberty movement for a generation, and justifiably so it would seem, given the accolades at her wake. She had also been one of the co-founders of the cult—along with Bobby Riley.

Lucy, when she finally got out of bed, found a reflective Bobby indeed.

"What's the matter with you? You look like shit!" She joked, usually able to get a bite from her companion. Not this time however. Bobby was too far gone to take heed of her mate's jocularity. Lucy soon gave up and went outside for a smoke of her own.

Out the front it was a Saturday morning and everyone was either mowing their lawns or hiring some Island Indigenous to mow it for them. A drone filled the air. Lucy had soon had enough and after stubbing out her butt on the window-ledge trod back inside to find Bobby pouring her umpteenth cup of coffee.

"Are you hungry?" No answer. Lucy made a cursory inspection of the fridge and cupboards for something that could pass for a breakfast but soon gave up, mostly because she wanted to get out of there anyway. "I'm going to McBurgers for a meal. Do you want to come?" At this Bobby floated back into focus and stuttered, "No, you go ahead, I want to do a few things here." Lucy was past caring and past hearing. She shook her head and went.

Jumping into her VW she putted off down the avenue, car belching black filth. Lucy jammed the windows shut in order to breathe a smidgeon of presentable air.

She drove quickly past the lawn-mowing maniacs marching up and down in columns. She drove 'flat tack' past girl-guides selling assorted biscuits door-to-door, past born-again Baptists peddling Bibles, past tough boys with tattoos and big biceps who wore cheap plastic wrap-around shades and sneered at you if you came too close to looking at them too closely, past old ladies with stolen shopping carts piled high with paraphernalia that was meaningless to everyone but them—and probably to them too.

She pulled up as the lights turned red.

The VW throbbed and the oil pressure light blinked on to 'real bright' and Lucy knew she had better feed it some Cost Less oil as soon as possible or she would be up 'shit creek without a paddle' as her brother used to say. So, when she could go again, she sped across the intersection and up a ramp into the nearest service-station where she asked a boy to check the oil and water while she went inside the kiosk to rummage through the newspapers, hoping to find one that didn't just have pictures of Governor Generals or Members of Parliament or rugby players splattered goon-like all over its front-page; that actually had something half-way intelligent to say. That wasn't an easy task, let me tell you, as the media was all written by the same person in the same script in every country in the world. There was no news anymore, only a façade. It was a story-book cartoon cut-out diorama. Real people had died off long ago. We were all (Lucy, you and me included) in a sort of postmodern stage show: a review of a boy-scout revue that no one took seriously. The news was fiction and fiction was the news.

What made it all so much worse, mused Lucy, as she tapped her fingers on the dashboard, was that violence and 'things' seemed to be the only 'newsworthy' items. People seemed to have vanished. Humanity had been deconstructed into statistics: *A gunman today killed 35 people* a billboard blared. Underneath, Lucy could just make out: *This sets a new record in the history of mass-murders by a single perpetrator on a weekday.* People were buying the bloody newspaper for no reasonable reason at all.

Lucy paid for her litres of crude black stuff, started up the Beetle, and plunged off back down the road in search of nibbles. Shit, she was ravenous, and still the lawnmowers continued their resilient hum.

65

At McBurgers it was weekend morning chaos. Freckle-faced kids, black, white and yellow, with assorted hues in between, were imploring reluctant parents and psuedo-parents to buy this and that, that and this—all plastic crap that was deliberately designed to splinter, snap and corrode so that the demand for the next media driven 'you've-got-to-have-this' campaign would continue ad-infinitum. Every kid wanted the latest gimmick and each gimmick was crazier than the one before. 'Get Supa Aktion Man who can divide into three parts simultaneously and disappear up its own arse at the same time. Self-replicating, self-cloning, self-creating. Only at McBurgers, the Home of Fun. Yunoit!' Lucy felt like puking, and she hadn't eaten there yet.

She shoved her way past piles of sweating mothers and mothers' mothers, past weekend fathers holding on for dear life to Tim, Hone and Hyacinth; past lost tots screaming for potato chips; past scrimmages of seven year-olds fighting like fuck over who owned the latest Supa Aktion Man, and sat down at an end plastic table which was in the shape of a giant peanut. The in-house radio blared out Donny and Maree—or perhaps their Asian twins—singing a pile of shit about 'Love All Summer Long' as the big McBurgers figure with the chronically insane/inane smile glared down at her. Lucy was reminded of the days when she was a child and her own father had taken her—hand-in-hand—through the mazes and dazes of the Easter show. She had felt an acute alienation then 'I don't fucking belong with this crowd,' and she still felt it now.

She ate dispiritedly, disconsolately, and alone, shutting-out the idle chit-chat about the next big film actor and the latest sports hero that was going on next to her. She stuffed the cardboard that was the burger into her mouth and jammed the rubber chips into the nether regions of her jaws, trying to ignore their taste. She needed to get out of Dirty City, and fast. She needed a new life. Not in the VW though, that was for sure. Its impending demise wasn't far away. She sighed, swung the rusting car door closed and headed downtown to the bus station. She had packed days ago, and Bobby would soon find out. Lucy couldn't face another ownership session. Already she felt a bit better, given the huge fast 'food' bilge weighing her down. The aftertaste was vile, but thoughts of escape mollified her.

*

Bobby Riley had crashed really early, even by her aging standards. The sun discovering some nooks and crannies had wedged its way into her house, the thin warmth numbing her drowsy sentience. She was soon snoring head-down on the kitchen table surrounded only by stained coffee cups and sugar spills. It would be hours before she woke to find her lover gone. She didn't notice the procession—a ceremony outside her bedroom window, people in an elongated march walking quietly along her street, a coffin at the tail-end of the queue.

It was a funeral, under the high, solemn sun—the people were on their way to a church at the far end of the road, near the intersection, which nestled serenely against a small yard dotted with tombstones. Far from Bobby Riley's rhythmic snores the snake twisted, oh so very slowly. None of the pallbearers—engrossed in their own steady dance—spotted her through the window either. Eventually they made it to the chapel, where turning inwards, they shut themselves out of sight.

Bobby, for her part, could not hear the frail wafts of singing along with the faint drips of organ chords that wound their way upwards from the alter. Then, no sounds at all. Just a solemn pall. No-one anywhere. Just one brief scream coming from somewhere in the sweaty day and a tired woman fast asleep in her cluttered kitchen.

*

In another part of Dirty Inner-City Doc was reading the morning paper with some interest. He had a fascination with the sports of the skinny country and was patriotic about his nation's team efforts against fatter nations. He skimmed a story about the local football team and their last-minute win over their traditional sporting rivals across the channel. Then smiled to himself, not because the grammar and the praxis of the piece were poorly put together, but because the skinny country had triumphed.

Doc had several degrees from various universities hanging on his wall, some of them in Imperialist Composition and Critical Writing. He knew all about epistemes and cultural capital, differance and hyper-reality, but Doc was able to compartmentalize all this jargon and the menace it meant for his day-to-day life—away from his day-to-day life. He could comprehend and rationalise the absurdity of his own logocentric nexus, but at the same time nourish it with junk food while watching stupid movies about idiots like himself. Mind you, Doc wasn't that much of an idiot on the Grand Scale of Idiocy. He was well on the way there, but—by fuck in all its glory—there were a few million greater contenders out there for the crown.

He hauled himself up out of his armchair as he heard the backfire of a beat-up old VW being push-started by a couple of Island Indigenous scavengers outside, then pausing, he admired his handsome visage in the mirror. He smiled and reflected 'David Graham, Dr David Graham, you're not a bad looking bastard.' He let out a 'silent sam' and sunk back down into his armchair to read a bit more about the football Kings. Outside the lawnmowers were having a field day. Field day. Get it?

*

It was raining again and Te Neke was sick. Sick of the weather, sick of the hassles. He slumped further into the front seat. He didn't want to think for a while, he just wanted to recoup his senses. Kick-start his mission. He still had a sore head, not so much from the glancing blows he had tried to escape in the carpark the other night, but because he might have been ripped off. He had handed a large part of his stash over to Hemi who insisted that only he could get the deal 'set'. Te Neke had no reason to mistrust his cousin, but then again, he hadn't seen Hemi after the scrap. Before it all blew up Hemi had come back from the 'deal man' and winked, and given him the nod as if to say that he had the money ... then it was all on.

From his vantage point from around the back of the carpark, where he had luckily gone for a piss, he saw the cops take away a couple of the boys screaming at each other like they were still on a primary school playground. He saw Sucker and Matipo zoom off into the night, full blast. Hadn't seen Matipo's lady friend though. Hadn't noticed Hemi either, although Fat Man told him that he thought he had seen Hemi 'bugger off' on his chopper some time before. 'Fuck it,' he mused, 'I'll get those bastards soon enough.' He still had a fair bit of his crop left, he was no fool, trouble was it would mean backtracking and he didn't want to waste more time.

NINE

Zita Parāone saw the long-haired bearded guy come out to the car park and take a lingering piss just a few metres from her. He looked stoned and didn't seem to see her. Quite a looker for all that. Reminded Zita of one of her cousins from the other side. Maybe he was. He had stumbled back into what would soon become a massive free-for-all—silly bastard.

From the safety of the truck cabin as it sauntered out onto the main highway, away from Matipo and his fists, she watched the cops arrive. The driver had looked a bit startled when she had sprung from nowhere and asked to hitch a ride. But, no problem, even though she was a bit battered and had a big bloody tattoo across her chin. 'What the hell,' thought Jimmy Norcliffe, who ran his own trucking company up and down the length of the skinny country, 'she looks like she needs a hand.'

Besides, he had nothing against tattoos. He rolled up his shirt-sleeves in the cab to counter the heatwave. 'I love Jo' was plastered over one of his biceps inside a rudimentary heart. Zita sighed and fell fast asleep as the sirens waned in the background.

*

Lucy got off the bus several kilometres past the last vestige of civilization. There were no houses or shops, only farm machinery and milk trucks zooming by. She stood uncertainly, not knowing where to head, as if the momentum of the bus had been her sole rationale. She lit a cigarette but soon stubbed it out on a fencepost as the bitterness rankled in her guts. Why had she taken up smoking? She didn't understand herself—something to do with role-modeling herself on Bobby Riley who had seemed so 'au fait', so suave and cool, so fucking knowledgeable about everything.

Lucy looked around but saw only a few brazen cows nearing as if to chew her ears off. Verdant tufts of grass sticking out of their bovine mouths like green whiskers. They smelt bad.

It wasn't going to rain, hadn't looked like rain for months. Much of the skinny country was going through a long—very long—dry spell. And it was hot, always so fucking hot. One of the cows dropped a huge slimy turd inches away from Lucy's feet on the inside of the barbed-wire fence as if to say "Whadd'ya think of that?" So Lucy trundled further away down the line of pastures as another massive milk-tanker roared by, setting off vibrations that bounced her up and down for several seconds and brought home to her the fact that she was very alone out there, and unprotected. For all her possessiveness, Bobby Riley had been a protector 'par excellence', just as long as you didn't contradict her.

Lucy trudged on a little way. Women, anyone, alone on the roads of the skinny country were not safe—day or night. All sorts of strange bastards were out there, preying on anything, including each other. There were vast cabals of internecine semi-subterranean networks riven through the fabric of the skinny country, buying and selling 'illegality' in every way, shape or form. Machinations often with the veneer of respectability. One never knew if one had bought a 'legitimate' article, was speaking to a 'legitimate' representative or a fraudster. Everything was mixed-up, a blur, a pastiche. Bricolage unbidden. After a sweaty slog up steamy seal Lucy saw a faded sign on the road-front stating, 'Farmstay. Bed and Breakfast. All Welcome'. And under that was another smaller piece of hand-carved wood, pegged onto the larger one: 'Vacancy'.

Lucy found a driveway a little further up the road. It was pitted with potholes most of which were clogged with dirty water—despite the omnipresence of the sunshine. A long line of dead poplars lined one side and on the other side were a few headless bushes. She plodded up it hoping to find shelter and rest.

The farmhouse lay sprawled at the end of a broken cul-de-sac. Half of the spouting gone. The windows were desolate, dark and broken. Parts of the roof curled bottom-side up to leer at the sky. A few scrawny chickens chattered in front of the open door, fuelled by their own visions. Weeds and lank grass pierced the cobblestone path leading up to the entrance.

Lucy walked inside. The place was deserted, yet still with some semblance of order, not too much shit laying around, and some rooms—as Lucy explored languidly—seemed reasonably inhabitable. She walked through the house almost having to climb up sections of the floor (such was the pitch of it) in places, and putting her foot through it in others.

She sat down on an old worn sofa and leaned back. She would sleep here tonight.

*

Mahon was often prey to a recurring vision that Being and Nothingness were engaged in a perennial, colossal struggle. That Nothingness generally had the upper hand and Being had to fight for its survival—its very existence—at all times. There was no such thing as easy creation. Nothingness lurked everywhere and was waiting to gulp down Being in any way, shape or form that it could. True, there were fleeting occasions when Being broke through but these flashes were not enough to escape Nothingness for long, and besides which, Mahon had had no such victory for years now. He fleetingly—as he squinted out the corner of his left eye to espy the sign 'Marshlands Motel, 4 km'—remembered something to do with bright lights and a lifting of his whole entity, but this was an amorphous after-image, a mere rubbing after the foundry had closed. Speaking of which, he rubbed his eyes, for he was sleepy. And hungry. And sick to death of driving.

He pulled into the motel car park, shingle on rock, turned off the Zephyr's steadfast engine and sat back. He felt as if he could sleep for a month, but knew that in his unusual state that was unlikely—that he would only betray himself and end up doing something else entirely. Mahon was his own worse enemy. Eventually, he managed to scramble out of the vehicle and lunge his way toward the office. The room was uninhabited and Mahon soon grew bored with waiting. After flicking through a couple of magazines like *Native Woman's Home* and *Deep Sea Scuba Sports,* and after pressing the bell and calling out several times "Is anyone there?" each time louder and louder, he gave up and went to find something, anything that could steer him towards shelter, bed and food. A few cars shot past outside but no one looked likely to stop and help him in his enquiries. He walked around the premises but found no one. A skinny white cat shot past him as he approached its rubbish bin hide-out but that was the sum of existence he found.

Out the back was a larger building with double doors—something like the residence of the owner, perhaps. Mahon scrunched his weary way towards it.

"Hello ... is there anybody there?" He called, before wending his way through the entire abode. He covered the ground floor quite quickly, pausing to munch a few potato chips left in a packet on the top of the refrigerator. What about upstairs? Up he went. It looked like bedrooms up there, so he hesitated and called out his same refrain again. He listened—there seemed to be sounds coming from down the end of the hallway. Should he go on down there? Of course he shouldn't, but he did anyway. The bedroom door was slightly ajar and Mahon squinting could make out a couple fucking on the bed. The room was gloomy so Mahon wasn't sure of the genders of the couple—he could only see the swell of the buttocks of one cresting the lower limbs of the other. He withdrew, but there was no coitus interruptus on the bed.

'Fuck it,' thought Mahon, 'I'll find my own place to sleep in.'

So, after a bit more absent-minded dawdling around the motel, he did, in one of the corner units that was shaded by the canopy of a large native tree shedding its oblong leaves across the fore-court. Just as Mahon felt himself to be sinking, he glanced upwards. Standing by the door was a sil-houette. Mahon could not make out the sex, iden-tity, or face—could only make out a blackness, a darkness about the person. Whatever it was it seemed to be staring at him with liquid eyes. The eyes were white and the black hair had a sheen despite the dimness of the evening. Mahon tried to talk to it but his sleepy voice was ineffectual gib-berish that sounded unclear, impractical and silly, even to his own ears. The figure never responded except through its eyes, staring—boring huge holes into Mahon. Once more Mahon shook his head, vig-orously this time, then looked back up. The staring figure had vanished. He called out like a jungle ani-mal. There was nothing. Mahon wiped his forehead vociferously. He wondered who this slim dark fig-ure could be, but had no answers. Perhaps an itiner-ant like himself, with no fixed abode, no place to go. Another drifter aimless on the edge of life, tangen-tially following some obscure arc—perennially.

Mahon soon was sleeping the sleep of a dead man: uninterrupted and motionless. You will have noticed, mes ami, that Mahon sleeps better the more this little tale unfolds. Sleep was bliss for Mahon. He had always enjoyed his sleep, always felt better after hours and hours of it. If there was one thing that Mahon had been really good at, it was sleeping. It was his panacea. More than an escape it was a different world he visited in other guises, and it all seemed to make so much more sense than his waking sphere.

In fact, I also feel like a little snooze right now and when I look around me Lucy is fast asleep in her farm-stay bedroom; David Graham has dropped off for a nap in his resolute armchair; Bobby Riley is snoring on the kitchen table after not sleeping much the night(s) before; Zita is firmly entrenched in the land of nod; Te Neke has slumped into a fitful doze while McWilliams is snoring out the back somewhere. Tamati—well, fuck knows where he is actually. And Molly is reclining under the front seat of the mighty Zephyr—itself having a bloody good rest outside. Only Dr Dallas is keeping an eye on things, but then again, that's his job requirement.

See you in the morning. And now some pictures to keep you occupied. They haven't got anything much to do with any of this, but—hell's bells—you guys are paying too much for this mess of shit anyway, so you've got to get something for your money, eh! Besides which, there's nothing much else here for me to do. I seem to have lost value for my gaolers—they are after fresher game now.

Quite good really arn't they? I will put in some photographs later on too.

Appendix One: Mahon's Dream.

Mahon was once employed in a vast labyrinthine abattoir in a mixed-race suburb. This was when he was first married and already a father, and many years before any university notions sprang to mind. When he had had to work to eat and to feed his whanau.

He secured a position on the mutton chain, way

down at the end where he trimmed pizzles. His workmates were fellow Indigenous like himself, many, newly arrived Island Indigenous with only a smatter of imperialist lingo, and none of Mahon's own mother tongue. Communication with them often consisted of gestures, growls and grimaces.

Mahon's recurring dream was a rehash of many mingled events from his lengthy spell on the mutton chain—a sort of a stew of second-hand bits and pieces served up after its use-by date.

It went something like this:

It was always wet, severely wet up there on the killing floor. Gumboots and silly white plastic aprons were the order of the day. Silly, because they didn't keep anyone dry, and their ties always became bedraggled and broken. And bloodied. Mahon is dank and trembling in the humid air that is caused by the continual sterilization process blowing up fetid wafts of wet spume, and from the knife canisters which emit steam.

He feels wetter than normal because, as he looks around, and peers into the steam, spray and blood, he can see a hose playing all over him. The hoser wetting Mahon is a hirsute young Island Indigenous, curly locks unencumbered by the silly hair net perched on them like a jester's cap. He grins broadly in glazed insouciance as he powers water in a steady arc over Mahon who cannot concentrate on his pizzles. Mahon begins to yell at this clown, but his words are drowned by the mindless hubbub of screams and yells of dying sheep, and men, and angry bosses (of the later almost all of whom are Caucasians with splotchy red-blue visages and broken noses) and a mongrel collection of machinery which screeches its despair at having to be there and which throbs raucously above the most ardent of the human voices. A mélange of the living and the dead, and the dying, fermented with a crescendo of whirring technical dervishes. Add a few thousand litres of water and blood and you see Mahon knee-deep in his nightmare.

He keeps on yelling, by now absolutely saturated and flaying his arms in a windmill fashion at the hoser, who grins asininely and stomps in the widening pink puddles in his new white gumboots which are far too big for him.

Others stop to stare and laugh. A couple of free-agents who can move from their non-chain gang duties, like meat inspectors and/or foremen, as well as other idiot hosers begin to gather around. Mahon by now is screaming so loudly that he wakes up. Bewildered and bedraggled.

TEN

Life had not been fair to him—Xavier fully believed. How was it that he was not as successful as some of his peers? Like that bastard Mahon who had gotten a good university job and was always getting published—although he hadn't heard from

80

or about Mahon for aeons now. Frances Xavier hit his clenched fist on his thigh in exasperation. OK, he had not gone on and achieved a successful post-graduate qualification, and had enrolled and dropped out again, on a number of occasions, but why was it people like Mahon had done so well? He knew why.

He hit himself, harder this time, because not only was he frustrated about his under-achieving in life, but also because the bloody gun was jammed and he was sick of ramming the bolt home and having to hold it in position to fire the damn thing. He couldn't afford a new firearm, or even a decent second-hand one. His part time job as a barman and dogs-body at the Existentialist Arms had only enabled him to scrape together enough for this piece of shit. As for his daily rut of selling poultry and assorted other products for Eggleton and Sons—that wasn't even worth thinking about. He sometimes felt—on bad days—that the hens were treated better than him.

Still, he could always go back to school-teaching!

Frances Xavier nearly choked in his rising vomit at the very thought of this.

Finally, as dusk broke over the horizon he managed to get off a couple of high-calibre shots, the recoil stung his hands and shoulder as his glasses plummeted to the clay bank below. He nearly hit the dark cardboard target on the tree too.

*

From the surveillance helicopter Jimmy Norcliffe's truck was a steady streak on the rarely-used, dusty highway that ran the length of the skinny country. Jimmy had been driving for what seemed like days. He had picked-up and dropped-off a curious raft of characters on his way, but now was driving on alone. Far, far away on the horizon was a large chimney spewing out black, noxious-looking fumes. The outlines of the gargantuan factory became clear as he approached.

Apart from this grandiose monster emitting its puke upwards there were no other buildings in sight. The landscape was more lunar than earthly: barren boulders scattered about unfenced paddocks. Jimmy could see no vehicles, nor any sign of human activity. He knew it to be an arms manufacturing plant, scarped by high electric barbed-wire fences. A dog sniffing around the fringes of the plant was the only sign of life. Some protestors—those few still able to roam free in the skinny country—knew of its existence, but had no potency to prevent its ceaseless chatter.

After a lengthy security check Jimmy handed over a sealed order form to some grinning marionette sitting behind the counter and watched as robots loaded his truck.

*

Mahon slept for a day or two. Oddly, no one seemed to enquire as to why his behemoth vehicle straddled the vestibule around the motel, nor did any cleaner, owner, used-car salesman, religious freak, prostitute, madman-qua-village-idiot, vacuum-cleaner merchant, dogcatcher, webpage wizard, girl-guide, homosexual-rights campaigner, market researcher, repairman or stray piddling dog seem to want to impinge on his lengthy slumber. It was one of those generously healing snoozes whereby one never really attains full consciousness, is never hungry, doesn't require a piss, let alone a number two—where one's entire metabolism rests.

When he woke up he felt a little more coherent. He farted and jumped into a hot shower. He wanted to wash away as much of himself as he could, turning on the water full-bore so that soon steam had over-ridden everything. The mirror soon vanished as well as the reflection of the hirsute man peering dopily into it. The taps plunging the room into mist also departed in the haze. Mahon had to strip in steam, feeling his way awkwardly towards the shower and through the cheap plastic curtain wrapping itself like limp octopuses around his out-stretched hands.

Inside the water burned like shit. His skin soon felt as if it was being flayed off in thin painful strips. Needle-point prickings penetrated his scalp like surgeon's pincers. His eyes stung with heat. When he turned around the pain in his penis caused by the scalding shot him back around to facing backwards to the torrent. It was lovely. Mahon found the torture cathartic. The caustic whippings on his body were revelations. The sheer agony of the over-ripe spume purged the skinny brown man standing unsteadily beneath the spray. Washing away the old Mahon.

Walking out into the cold room revived Mahon even more. He remembered grainy black and white television pictures of mad Europeans running naked from snowbound saunas into the snow—laying and rolling in its icy clutches like dogs in a dust bath. The chill slammed his perspiring, fervid skeleton into a hasty revitalization, even if only briefly. Contrarily, it also enervated him, and he was soon recumbent again, snoring like a snake, lying naked on the motel bed—lost, oblivious, and alone.

*

Lucy was raped by 'Uncle' Dick when she was 14. She had wanted to kill the bastard. 'Uncle' Dick was no blood relation—just a dirty old man who needed a fucking bullet. She was raped more than once too—several times over a few years.

Lucy had no mother to speak of—her 'Aunty' Pat had brought her up and 'Aunty' Pat was a loser in her own sweet way. 'Aunty' Pat was terrified of 'Uncle' Dick and the hidings he regularly administered, so she always tried to avoid confrontations. She conveniently overlooked Lucy's complaints that Dick had touched her inappropriately, and ignored Dick's punishment sessions which involved smacking bare bottoms and then penetrating a good deal further with more than his hand.

What was all the more sickening to Lucy, was that Dick and Pat were so-called evangelists and attended local church services most Sundays. Dick was a staunch member of the local RSA and Pat prided herself on her membership to Mothers United for Christ. Lucy managed to shut out the memories, most of the time, it was only on occasions like now that she started recalling them.

The car into which she had clambered after her first hassle-free hitch-hikes was travelling way too fast, and the driver was talking far too crazily for her liking. He had funny looking eyes and his mouth was too big for his head, while his beard looked fake. He slobbered on about 'bloody bitches' and 'typical slut behaviour' in his oddly cadenced accent, at the same time chain-smoking, as they progressed further into the rural interior of the skinny country.

'Uncle' Dick had also 'sped up' when he was about to fuck her in her bedroom, well after lights were out, and 'Auntie' Pat—ostensibly—was asleep. Dick would ramble some rattlesnake rubbish and then seize her and use her like something disposable. This funny-looking driver guy was beginning to worry Lucy, for he too was prattling incessantly and semi-incoherently. Faster and faster. Driving and talking. Funny how nonsense parallels speed. And how everything seems to have become so much quicker these days, eh.

Lucy felt for the door handles, which fortunately for her, were there—she knew of one of her mates who had been seated in such a misadventure and had found no door handles with which to escape. All that she wanted now was a couple of minutes of slower motion and a distraction. She retrieved her bag from the backseat in an effort to fool the frenetic driver into believing that she was searching for a smoke. She grasped it closer to her body and waited for the right time. Trouble is, the road had no stopping points—it was a highway repeating on itself for kilometre after boring kilometre.

Lucy decided to provoke a response from the man, to accelerate the situation.

"What's the next town, please?"

"Why?"

"I need to stop and get a few things ..."

"Why? We've got everything we need right here—sounds, speed, smoke ..."

"No, I need a beer or two."

The manic man blinked and actually slowed himself and the car somewhat. "Yeah," he said, "that's not a bad idea." Maybe he was thinking this 'girl' would be easier than he thought, you know, get her pissed, get her laid, eh. He guffawed. "Blank Junction."

"What?" Said Lucy.

"Is the name of the next town. Blank Junction."

"How far?"

"About 15 kilometres ... good pub there too. Play pool?"

"Yeah, I do actually."

"Haha," he said and put his foot down onto the floorboards.

They remained as they were, each envisaging their own respective chances when they got there. Mohammed Ayahab bin Noham, the driver, was mind-masturbating. Lucy was thinking about carrying a gun in future.

ELEVEN

God certainly moved in mysterious ways though, thought Frances Xavier, as he studied the front pages of the regional newspaper prior to getting out of his sweaty front-seat. The Indigenous masses were getting away with far too much these days. It hadn't always been that way, though. When he had been growing up in the backstreets of the city, a good Indigenous was an inconspicuous one.

Now everywhere he went in the city were multicoloured human forms. All sorts from all ports. Jabbering and jibbering in multifarious tongues. Dressed in exotic attires. Dragging extraordinary retinues of look-a-like little ones behind them. "Lord," and here he crossed himself in devout devotion as a mark of his unriven faith, a gesticulatory habit he had had inscribed deeply in him during his strict primary school upbringing at the convent of St. Thomas the Doubter, "you have sent all this to try us. You have granted wealth and fame and—worse still—publicity, to infidels and foreigners. You have elevated assorted Indigenous to the ranks of politicians, financiers and academics.

You have granted unlimited entry to an array of heathen exiles to our shores. They can't even speak our language." Here, he shifted yet another crate of Number Ten Browns into place at the back of the small delivery van before hoisting the eggs onto his shoulder so as to better carry them inside the Gaoxing Splendid Restaurant Emporium Limited. "But I have faith in your ways. I will continue to fight the good fight, despite the mystic obscurity behind your actions."

At this he lumbered the goods through the low slung rear door of the eatery and feigned a smile as a slim dusky boy with an invisible moustache and matchstick arms signed the papers in an indecipherable coda.

Once, he had seriously thought about entering the seminary, but had never got around to it, could never summon enough self-conviction to do so. He had gone two paces forward and ever three steps back. No, his calling, he was convinced, was in ensuring God's will here in the netherworld of the polyglot Hell in which he now scrambled a miserable living. He patted down the few remaining wisps of greying hair on his spreading bald pate and slammed shut the van's back doors as a robust sign that he had finished this particular delivery, and would not be back there again this week.

*

Mahon, unsurprisingly, slept on.

Tamati was at a hui that day. Being kaumātua he was behoven to say a karakia or two, so he did. Here is one of them:

E te mātou matua
Kua ruia nei o purapura pai
Homai i koe he ngākau hōu
Kia tupu ake ai
E Īhowa
Kaua a tukua
Kia whakangaromia
Me whakatupu ake ia
Kia kitea ai ngā hua
Āmine

If only Mahon was listening, because these words were particularly relevant to him in his present condition. But no, he was snoring away on bright yellow eiderdown while that rapscallion sun browned down on everything outside, trying always, ever always, to get into the room through any possible chink.

Bobby Riley was past prayer. Thought God had died years ago. Maybe 'He' did too. She had made a couple of phone calls to powerful figures nevertheless. Lucy wasn't going to get away that easily. She may not have been a member of the Cult, but she couldn't be allowed to escape its clutches either.

*

Carlos Te Neke was getting annoyed with the way the weather kept on changing. No sooner had he switched off the windscreen wipers and succumbed to the wanning sun's shafts, than it began to drizzle all over again.

He had found Hemi. Hemi reckoned that "yeah, he got the bread off that fucker Sucker," but that he in turn "had been ripped off by another fella," one Jake Heke, whom Te Neke had never heard of and who sounded like someone ripped from the pages of a novel. Te Neke was beyond pissed off, he was fucking wild. He saw red, quite literally. His spectrum of vision suffused to a raging glow. He dealt to his cousin 'big-time' in a school playground, in the middle of the skinny country, where he had tracked down Hemi after noticing his bike outside a tavern, and after their mooching over to the field ostensibly to have a puff or two.

One thing was for sure, Hemi didn't have any dope or much money now. After Te Neke finished with him, he only had one and one-half ears left too. And his once proud beard was half-torn from his face. No matter if he was Te Neke's whanau—he had messed up big-time. Carlos hadn't heard a man scream like that ever before. Far worse than a stuck pig. He could have been heard for miles around if there had been anyone there.

Te Neke wiped his knife on Hemi's jacket and climbed back into his Valiant. He would get his money one way or another.

"Shit," he expectorated out of the window as he

lurched off. Out of the corner of his shaded eyes he was certain he glimpsed Dun Mihaka parading a whakapohane up the side of the road. Knew his arse from all the wanted posters displayed everywhere. If he had had time he would have stopped to catch up.

The bloody sun was out again—full-bore, bearing down, baring all.

*

David Graham was awake now and preparing a meal for himself in his up-market kitchen. He was hungry after his hard day in the office, farting and lolling around on his armchair, sleeping and watching soap operas on his wide-screen television. What was in the cupboards today?

David Graham had been married once—to his childhood sweetheart, Sue—although she hadn't reciprocated his feelings till a considerable time later. They had a daughter to show for it. Both then worked all day and both liked pretty things that cost a fair bit. Sue had loved him at first and put up with his self-obsessive ways, then she started to grow tired of him. Then they decided to part ways before they really began to despise each other. David Graham had become sick of her too. She went awol one day after shunting her daughter Sue off to her mother's.

That was a few years back. Now David Graham preferred to go to massage parlours to fuck. He could afford to. That—plus wanking a fair bit—was probably why he was so tired. David Graham spent a fair bit of time playing with himself. And looking into the mirror. And doing both of these things at the same time. He was a self-voyeur. And solipsistic to an extreme degree. He pulled out some beans and bacon and cooked them up. He could eat whatever the bloody hell he felt like, whenever he wanted to. That was the plus side of being a wealthy 'single white male' with few obligations, or worries.

After dinner he sat back down and watched TV— something about a gumboot throwing competition down the skinny country somewhere ....

*

In Blank Junction there was no policeman, no fire-man and no security guards. Only the obligatory hotel, a corner dairy and a gas station that was part of both. Johannes Blank had come from Europe last century and had developed the place: thus the name, although there is also no doubt that it was living up to its appellation—the place was one step removed from a corpse.

When the car pulled into the decaying petrol sta-tion and a fat white woman wearing a dress from sixty years ago and about six times too small for her appeared to 'serve' them, Lucy fled the fuckwit who was edging inevitably towards raping her. She ran through the dairy and out into an odd area, which seemed to be made up of old cricket bats nailed together to form outhouses. She pried open the lattice on the window of one and snuggled inside, on a layer of dusty old sacks which someone had forgotten about, about twenty years ago. She lay silently, hoping that the clown would give up and drive on.

Soon, however, she heard voices—a whiny woman's nasal screech and the familiar snarl of the driver. The tones drew close for a while and then vanished gradually. Later—maybe half an hour or so further into the heat—Lucy thought that she heard a car drive off. She waited for another few minutes and then summoned up enough oomph to go and see if he had really gone.

Out front there was no one. Lucy glanced in each direction and soon realized she no longer had a sex-starved whacko to contend with—at least not that day. She relaxed and went inside the dairy where the fat woman was watching some asinine television soap about sex crimes.

It seemed compulsory for such places as Blank Junction to have old, red-faced people serving behind the counter: people with tired figures, muttering tongues and scowling looks who seemed uncomfortable in these retail outlets—didn't want to be there, and, even more, didn't seem to want any customers there either. These people were like barnacles on the sides of rotting hulks and Lucy sensed they scuttled away when she left, back into their dark little hollows inside their dark little buildings.

So, this dour geriatric said, "Oh, there you are, dear. Don't worry, he's gone now."

"Yeah—he was a fucking creep."

93

"Yes, dear, when you vanished like that I guessed you weren't keen on him. He had awful breath too. Smelled like he ate garlic all day."

"He had no fucking door handles in his car," Lucy lied for effect ... "you got a smoke, by chance?"

The fat woman wearing the child's dress threw an open packet of El Cheapo cigarettes towards Lucy, who grasped them fervidly and took her fix.

"Yeah, I had to bullshit him, you know dear ... I told him that I knew you and that you were probably on the phone to the coppers. Ha, he shot off after that, yunno."

The fat lady whose name was Sue smirked and made a cup of tea. Lucy liked her. Sue had been in Blank Junction, "Since Christ was in Nappies." Had had a few men, wink wink nod nod, but had got sick of the silly bastards who only wanted to sleep, fuck and eat. "Bloody waste of time." Now she ran the triumvirate of enterprises alone, which scratched out a sort of living for her. She met up with her grandchildren a "cuppla times a year" and that was that. Her "bloody daughter, got my name, but no damned good, always roaming around," and her, weren't on speaking terms. Maybe Sue wasn't so dour, actually, Lucy later mused.

Lucy stayed out the back in one of the psuedo-latrines for a couple of days before it was time to move on. Sue threw her a bit of wisdom the morning Lucy decided to slip away.

"One piece of advice, dearie. Keep a knife in your bag. If one of those bastards tries it on again, stab him in the cock. It'll stop him right in his tracks."

Lucy smiled and wished her farewell.

TWELVE

Mahon woke up in his usual bedazzled state. It took him a few minutes to work out where he was. Shit, he was hungry—and not only mo he kai. He was horny too—strange for a man clawing out from the depths of a depressive hangover. He wanted to fuck, and wanking into a motel bedroom mirror wasn't going to serve his purpose this time.

Before he went he turned the television on to the music channel. There was a replay of an old concert and on screen in full colour was Iggy Stooge singing (if that is the appropriate word) *I just wanna be your dog*. Mahon stood transfixed for a while, the song bringing back a flush of memories to him.

Then he heard screaming above Iggy. A thin anguished wail of horror rising up, higher and higher. "Jesus!" He crouched a little, listening, his whole body whitening as if in empathy with the terrible sound. He could not place exactly where the cries of anguish were coming from. He switched Iggy down low and listened some more. They seemed to be coming from quite some distance away, from out beyond the confines of the motel. Someone—there was no doubt here—was in dire peril. Mahon found himself outside, sprinting as fast as his flab would allow him, towards the screaming. It seemed to have subsided now, but he ran on as well as he could, feeling hot and bilious as his body procrastinated, sputtered and overheated in the vindictive sun.

He was soon jogging through a large space which resembled a park. He couldn't see anything ahead. The screaming had ceased. He stood, panting rapidly, looking everywhere. Finally, he slumped to the ground, a physical wreck, feeling sick and old, tired and worn, smelly and useless. His left hand felt damp and as he looked down he spotted blood spots on the grass between his fingers. Someone or something had been sliced up here very recently. The blood was profuse.

He slouched back to his trusty steed and his traitorous body reminded him that it wanted sex—not to run around like an idiot.

With that in mind, he drove out of the uninhabited motel and sought more lively game.

Back on the road he glanced into his rear vision mirror and noticed a car following his own. A large machine like his, but, because of its facsimile tinted glass, Mahon could not get a glimpse of its occupants, nor could he ascertain just how long the car had been behind him. He hadn't sensed its presence at all. Tail-gating. Slipping along in Mahon's slipstream— doppelganger giants.

A little further ahead some sort of procession was coming towards them—as Mahon approached he realized it was a funeral tail in the middle of nowhere. Odd. He hadn't noticed cemeteries, churches, or any habitations for kilometres. But a funeral it certainly was: about eight or nine cars, all with their lights on, following a large hearse driven by a bearded man wearing a dark suit and dark glasses.

By the time he had passed the strange parade the car in the rear vision mirror had disappeared.

Around the next few bends were signs strung out at frequent intervals. WELCOME was the first one—a word resplendent in itself. Then came TO, followed symmetrically by NIRVANA.

Nirvana, when he reached it, was little more than a cattle-town strung along the highway like sheep droppings. The Piesteak Bar sounded promising though, so Mahon halted his vehicle outside and strode on in, only to hear ruinous country wailings from some morose man who *had sent his love aaw-waaaaay.* "Fucking hell," mused Mahon. Still, he bent over the counter and squinted up at the menu written in handwriting high above.

'Pie-steak Meal – $10 Special Today.'

Mahon had to try this. If only for the experiment.

Actually, it tasted pretty bloody good.

He licked his lips and asked for a second cup of coffee. He soon noticed a young woman in the far corner reading a newspaper and staring into space at the same time. She—from his myopic distance—looked pretty to him, so he sat back and thought up ways to approach her. His penis twitched. He watched her for a while before deciding that he couldn't think of any credible approach whatsoever.

Then she approached him for a light. Mahon

didn't smoke, not even much dope of late, so couldn't oblige, but remembered that he had seen a basket of book-matches up on the counter. So, he said to the woman, "wait a moment," got off his backside, fetched a book and lit her cigarette.

They struck up a spasmodic conversation—her between sucking in gouts of nicotine, him, because he couldn't think of anything cogent to say. It transpired that she was indeed Lucy and she was going to no place in particular. 'Join the club,' Mahon felt like saying, but didn't, because he thought he should sound more on to it than he actually was. Mahon got up again when Lucy said that the sounds in this place were crap. He walked over to the jukebox and found some Bob Marley amongst the dross. Soon the Piesteak Bar was jamming to 'Funky Reggae.'

Lucy thought the guy was quite cute. He seemed somewhat diffident and not a hard on, hard-on. Little did she know what was going on in Mahon's brain.

They talked about a few things—mainly music and artists, movies and artists, and writers and artists—and realized that they shared similar tastes. Bob Marley was soon followed by a soul singer with a caressing voice and more cups of coffee. No-one else was in Piesteak Bar that early in the day, except the intermittent owner / counter-attendant. So time passed, as it seems to do, and Lucy and Mahon found themselves quite attracted one to the other and they hadn't even been drinking alcohol. They decided to get in the Zephyr and drive a bit more that day. So they did. The Zephyr seemed to steer itself and Mahon turned the car stereo way up. Lucy was tranquil and her memories of Dirty City were fading fast. The open road beckoned and Mahon was cuter than ever.

Soon Nirvana was gone and they were flying along the highway—Janis Joplin singing to them alone. Lucy fell asleep and Mahon felt remarkably mellow. Janis was followed by Jimi as day disintegrated into night and still they drove on, further away from Dirty City and Bobby Riley, whom Mahon had once wanted to kill.

THIRTEEN

It had been another cruel day in the life of Frances Xavier. He had absentmindedly dropped an entire carton of Halals Yolky Yummy Yoghurt, the contents of which had messed the entire front floor of the Arab delicatessen where he was delivering it. The resultant glutinous stains over his overalls drenched his clothing underneath and he had stunk for the rest of the day—accentuated by the high dense heat from above. His balls had stuck to his inner thighs in a combustible raspberry morass and every time he moved a few pubic hairs got agonisingly ripped out.

He staggered home later than was usual for him, for he had been asked to explain the 'accident' to his immediate superior, Mr Ji, who informed him that he would have the losses debited from his monthly wage. Frances Xavier had had to call upon all of his inner strength not to leap across the thin bureau and strangle the living pulp out of his boss—especially as he could not decipher some of the man's vocabulary. Indeed, he seemed at times to be talking in tongues, and Frances Xavier was convinced that it was a deliberate ploy to keep him frustrated and confused. It didn't sound like the correct imperialist lingo of Frances Xavier's distant youth. It was easier to listen to machines these days.

Passing by his local grandiose media-shop, en-route to his apartment downtown, he glanced through a side window near the alleyway that led to the stairwell to his fourteenth floor council flat. There, among several other tomes lowered in price through their age and/or inability to be sold were several copies of *Me and Colin Wilson* by that fat buffoon David Graham. There was even a picture of the obese author on the front cover. Frances Xavier groaned inwardly. How had an incompetent like that ever managed to have a book published let alone remaindered? David Graham had always been larger than life, even when all three of them went to J.G. Hamman Memorial Technical College together. He thought briefly of his own attempts at publication and the piles of rejection slips he had received over the years. There was no justice in this world.

Before he could be admitted into the grey and grotty granite trunk that was and had been his abode for decades now, he had to prove who he was by presenting to the sterile machine that guarded the premises his computer-enhanced image enclosed on a laminated micro-chip card that everyone by law, now had to carry, embedded in their person. Frances Xavier still could not understand why he was allowed to access his own home only if he could show an ideal version of himself: a replica which had more verisimilitude than the original. He had been told that central government, wherever that was now, had a vast store of files with everyone's appearance numerically catalogued, however only technological images were accepted and 'real' photographs were not used. These images had been conjured up by some overseas derived software programme that used data from some other central agency, somewhere else.

He waved his fanciful image in front of the sensor and was allowed to carry his corpus up the stairwell. His plastic ideal, it would seem, had more existence than himself.

*

Jimmy Norcliffe paused for a time at a roadside cafe deep in the midriff of the skinny country.

He lurched back into the tepid day munching on a meat pie, staring. He saw a couple peering intently at his truck and then back at him. They were a strange enough looking pair, even to his hardened road eyes. One seemed to be a dwarf, or unnecessarily short, with a large bulbous head and protruding eyeballs which oscillated across his high forehead like some sort of zany computer. He was dressed in shorts and gumboots and across his eyes were wrapped thick black plastic spectacles, probably purchased from a $2 store. Jimmy was sure he had seen this swarthy guy somewhere before, possibly in a comic somewhere.

The other inquisitive youth was an apposite opposite. He looked rather like an elongated string bean, hollow in the middle, sunken-in like an inverted blowhole with huge gangly legs capped by brown plastic sandals. His waist matched the gnome's crown in height and he stretched way up into the sky, loose and unwieldy. Jimmy had not seen this chap in any comic—rather he looked like a steam roller had run him over, not once, but several times. As Jimmy strode over to mount his cab the odd couple parted to let him through.

"Howsitgoing?" Mumbled Jimmy through his mince.

"Good," volunteered the unshaven tall one, his voice drawn down from the clouds. "We were – er –wondering whether we could cadge a ride with you?"

"Howfaryougoing?" Muttered Jimmy.

"Not far. We've got relatives in the next town."

"Shit," thought Jimmy, "if these guys have got any relatives in the next town it must be a fucking zoo." Still, he relented, and let them slide into his side-seat.

"Onto the next town, then," he offered, as they drove out of that one.

It transpired that their names—or so they claimed—were Holt and Hunter, and they were local country boys who had been in the small town to do some business. Now they wanted to head home, but didn't want to wait for the infrequent bus.

Holt and Hunter said nothing but garbage about tractors and silos and milking sheds all the way along their mini-journey. There was something about their shared oddball articulation that disturbed Jimmy, who was aware that he was not meant to pick-up hitchhikers given his mandate of travelling incognito—as just another trucker. It was imperialist lingo spoken with a pronounced accent. These boys were sure as hell not from around here.

He slotted Hank Williams Senior into his CD and pretended to listen to their waffle, but really he had switched off and was concentrating on the road ahead. *I'm so lonesome I could cry*, lamented Hank.

Suddenly, Holt, or Hunter—one of the twosome—sung out that he needed a piss and could he, Mr Driver, stop please? The other half of the pairing also decided he wanted the same release, so Jimmy slowly eased over to the side of the road to allow them both to scamper out. But they did not pause, merely hopped over a fence and ran. He last glimpsed them disappearing from view over the brow of a small rise, his opened door swaying in the turgid breeze.

"Fuckin' nutters," he swore, shaking his head

as he pulled the door shut. He hoped that Holt or Hunter—or whatever their names were—never crossed his path again.

Hank Williams had finished and Jimmy couldn't see any more tapes on the floor. He felt around down there anyway and pulled out the only tape his fingers could find. The music, if it was that, seemed to be metallic and foreign, like an assemblage of spare parts jumbling around in a monstrous cement mixer. The sound was a cacophony of screams, whistles, chants and what sounded like chainsaws. His ears hurt as the white noise climbed upwards and then abruptly stopped.

It was only much later when he decided to halt for the night that he noticed the scrawny label on the tape, *Calls of the Mullah*. 'Sure as hell isn't mine,' he thought. He half expected to see Holt and Hunter lying in wait for him in the anonymous wayside he pulled into.

No, they were not there. The paddocks must have swallowed them up. Or a transient circus offered them lucrative contracts as clowns.

*

Away on the horizon Mahon saw a long flat plain and what seemed to be worker-ants bedevilling themselves in a hive of activity. There were scores of them running around and some construction seemed to be mounting in their midst. A vaguely semi-circular edifice in its first stages from what

Mahon could see. Lucy was asleep, slumped over the front seat next to Mahon.

As they drew nearer his initial visions were confirmed. A huge concrete monster in the shape of an open-air amphitheatre was rising above a horde of workmen scurrying about in overalls and workboots, carrying planks, concrete blocks and assorted building equipment. They were oblivious of Mahon's arrival—his huge car pulling into the driveway and his frazzled frame disembarking from it. They shouted orders to one another, whistled and sang—continuously on the move. Further away on the construction site small trucks zoomed about, while, as Mahon squinted upwards into the omnipresent sun, two gigantic cranes swung past with steel beams.

Mahon scratched his head in bewilderment at the frenetic activity—he had only stopped to have a crap. Lucy, by now, had woken up and was rubbing her eyes at the chaos. Constructing a massive building in the middle of nowhere, for no apparent commercial reason seemed insane. Yet, Mahon reflected, mankind seemed to be continually building monstrosities and knocking them down for no apparent reason.

He called out to the nearest workman, a large Indigenous with a full black beard who was clutching a wheelbarrow laden with concrete slabs. The fellow glanced towards Mahon, rather wild-eyed, then strode on towards the construction.

Mahon spat onto the ravaged earth. He then

called out to another passer-by—politely—but received the same rebuff. A conspiracy of mutes, perhaps. Very annoying. He was tempted to climb back into his car and zoom off but he needed a shit real bad. He turned to see Lucy winding down the window.

"I'm just going to find a toilet," he said, perfunctorily, as he had already set off to do just that.

Mahon could see a large dome stretching towards the clouds in the form of rotund scaffolding a few hundred yards away. He started walking in that direction, perhaps there would be a latrine inside, for there seemed to be no worker's facilities anywhere that he could spot. He had to sidestep several bustling workmen who, if he hadn't done so, would have bowled him over in their passage. It was a kind of bizarre dance, with no set steps except side-step, back-pedal, speed-up. Finally, he reached the edifice, incomplete but gaining volume by the minute. It was multi-storied and covered in glass windows, yet, from what Mahon had seen thus far, had no human ablution zone whatsoever. The concrete was still fresh and bright gray, the windows smeared with builders chalk, the grass outside nonexistent—merely dry soil specked with one or two thistles.

The irony was that, while men were zooming around outside of the building, very few were actually erecting on site. Mahon squinted at a doorway and then went eagerly towards it, for to his eyes it read 'TOILET.'

Actually, it spelt 'TO LET', which became apparent the closer he got, his arse full and his guts beginning to ache with the load. He pulled back the door anyway, half-expecting to see a toilet seat waiting for him, but all that was there was an old desk and some chairs scattered around the newly concreted floor. It was a worker's food-eating area, if the scraps of litter and a dust-bin overflowing with orange peel were any indication.

He walked towards another smaller door, which opened into a long, dim corridor. He was met by an almost deafening noise as he descended slowly into it. Indubitably, he was going underground. The passageway seemed interminably long and moronically circuitous. It wound down and around, down and around. The noise grew louder, more penetrating and chronic. The light grew gloomier and gloomier. The air colder and colder as Mahon became more and more apprehensive. 'What the fuck is this place?' He wondered to himself. The entire monstrosity was eerie. The din grew until Mahon could hear the whirrs and buzzes, growls and groans of what he imagined to be giant machines caressing each other. He had, by now, forgotten his urge to excrete.

Finally, he came to another smaller door, which he had to stoop through to get inside. Curiosity as much as anything was leading him on now. Mahon peered around in the half-light his ears shattered by the din. Steam rose everywhere, hissing wrathfully. He could see rows and rows of panels with little flashing lights—stacked several stories high. He could also see what seemed to be giant boilers chuffing away in the distance, while over on his left, huge cogs were churning around and around ceaselessly striking sparks off every circuit. As he looked around again he saw a gaunt grinning figure in a dusty black singlet striding towards him, in his hands a board and a pen. The figure had on safety glasses and was smeared in oil. Just as Mahon was about to speak—above the horrendous cacophony—the figure bypassed him and strode around the corner. Mahon was further baffled. The place was some kind of engine room, some giant central nervous system, although no one would have known of its existence from above ground—where Lucy incidentally was becoming frustrated and had started rummaging through Mahon's Zephyr looking for something to read, eat, anything—clumps of cables hung from the ceiling and smaller multicoloured wires shot in all directions, gathering here and there like party streamers. The steam continued to rise and the noise savaged his ears. The lights on the banks of panels flashed on and off whilst the boilers churned in mad rhythm. Mahon had been in some odd places, but this was one of the strangest he'd encountered.

The noise reached such a crescendo that Mahon felt as if his brain was splitting apart each time it peaked. Whoever had orchestrated this mélange of mayhem must be a raving madman. Mahon's head splintered and he sensed a monster headache coming on. His sphincter had forgotten why it had led him there and as he turned he realized that he had lost his way. He had to get out, now. He stumbled around until he found two huge roller doors descending slowly. He ducked through them just before he was decapitated—the din welling behind him like an insane tidal wave.

*

Lucy meanwhile had found an apple amongst the jetsam on the back seat and was munching it rather absentmindedly. Amongst the rubble she had also discovered a worn paperback novel, with its covers chewed up. It was rubbish, but she didn't mind as she skipped through its pages waiting for the guy with the woolly beard to come back. She was oblivious to the occasional workman who—dungareed and moustached—loomed up then dissipated back into the heat-haze.

The book was an obscure detective saga with no apparent title. Lucy settled back, chewing away, reading the yellowing pages. It was a D-grade thriller. Routine garbage which you could pick up in any second-hand bookshop. Strong central man—all action and no self-analytical puke. Luscious, buxom blondes whose prime predilection was sex and heaps of it. Fast cars, guns and violence. Lucy found herself smirking, then laughing out loud as she speared through the bland crap to where the 'hero' of the tale had to capture the villain, necessarily attired in black from head to toe. The hero carried a revolver, a snub-nosed European model with special-effects bullets, the type that killed via mutilation. The hero was closing in as Lucy sped through the pages lulled on by the promise of ultimate mayhem.

The hero drew close to the arch-villain and fired one, two, three shots, at point blank range. The bad guy's head jerked back, bits of scalp-tissue and teeth flying, blood spurting in torrents onto the mews' walls. The author of this adventure spared no details of the gore. Lucy read onto the denouement—her apple now mere core—herself less avidly involved after the bloodbath with the redistribution of stolen goods to their rightful owners, the incarceration of the lesser hoodlums, and the inevitable engagement of one of the blonde women to the hero. Lucy closed the paperback wearily, leant back and sighed— another dime novel by the prolific O. Rang.

Mahon—while this was going on—was doing his best to escape his conundrum. He had found himself in another dim—but level—corridor, which he followed for a while. He eventually came across a small, evilly-lit room where two bespectacled men dressed in greasy, oil-spattered overalls were bent over a low table, playing cards.

Mahon watched for a while, scratching his head until he could stand their silence no longer. "Hello?" He said. No response.

"Hello?" He tried, a bit louder. Still nothing. The two continued dealing. They seemed to play at break-neck pace, as if their lives were depending on the result. But the game seemed nonsensical to

Mahon. The two men played on and on, their noses almost touching the bent and dirty edges of the cards.

Mahon yelled, "How do you get out of this ..." and here he paused, "out of this er, place?" Still no response. He yelled again.

Finally, one of the two men noticed him. His attention came away from the mass of cards and briefly focused on the sweltering stranger.

"Out there, man," he said, sweeping his arm towards a corner of the room where there may have been a door. By the time Mahon turned back from the direction of the sweep to thank him, the man was enveloped in the card game again.

Mahon trotted—for by now he was a little worried about how long he had been gone from his car and his passenger—towards a small door that he hadn't noticed earlier. From underneath it a bright light spread into the room. He pushed at the handle in anticipation. A lofty passageway climbed steadily but surely upward. He sped along it until he came to a small thin door hinged to the side of the passageway. It looked like a closet door. How peculiar. He felt like Alice in Wonderland. Except this was more like an incubus than a fantastic dream. Mahon felt shattered—depleted in enthusiasm, resources and energy. He felt his frame was dwindling, evaporating—disappearing from existence. He would have screamed except that he felt his timbre would have been a mere squeak. He was edging towards panic. He pulled on the closet handle. After some effort the door swung open. Inside, seated behind what appeared to be a school desk, which straddled the entire width and depth of the closet, was another filthy man who seemed to be engrossed in counting little red buttons into piles.

He was so involved in this chore, that he was oblivious to the presence of Mahon. All of the staff Mahon had thus far encountered—if that's what they were—seemed to be workaholics. Pedantic to the point of absurdity. This last chap was no exception. He counted on and on, what looked to be thousands of little red buttons, into piles. Surrounding him were banks and rows of small computer screens.

Mahon slammed the door. How the fuck did that guy breathe in there? Did he breathe? Perhaps he was an automaton? Who knew? Mahon shrugged despairingly and walked on in his eccentric fashion. He seemed to be climbing slowly but surely upwards. The light becoming clearer all the time, but still, he could see no way out of this futile tunnel.

At long last a door—another bloody door—appeared on the horizon. Mahon could see clear blue skies through the glass, and shadowy figures scrimmaging beyond. As he yanked it open he could see that he was back in the lobby of the amphitheatre and that his massive Zephyr was close by.

Swerving to avoid a crazed forkhoist Mahon sprinted as fast as he could back to the car, reversed feverishly past semi-robotic helmeted clowns hacking away at a trench, and screeched onto the highway.

"That was a long toilet stop," said Lucy.

Mahon's explanation—jumbled, and to Lucy at least, incoherent—was enough to send her back to sleep. Mahon planted his foot on the accelerator in an earnest attempt to get as far away from the site as possible. Thoughts of a tutae were the furthest thing from his mind now. He still had no inkling as to what the edifice was for—if anything.

At dusk, Mahon espied another roadside inn, sort of lit-up, in that an outside light was on and there seemed to be some activity upstairs. He woke Lucy—more by his skidding onto the shingle and slamming his door than by any deliberate action. She peered dopily at him for a moment, before recalling who he was.

"Where are we?"

"Ummm, not sure," muttered Mahon, who didn't really care as long as there was food / bed / sleep / sex somewhere around. He farted quietly, in deference to his company. "Are you hungry?"

"S'pose so," she said, and angled her way out of the front seat of the car. They went inside.
They heard noises above them, something like footsteps in the distance, but no voices.

"Fucking hell," said Mahon, "another bloody deserted village."

"What?"

"Doesn't matter ... let's find some food."

They pushed through the swing doors into what seemed to be a restaurant area, though there were no tables and chairs—only a couple of stools by a

113

cane bar which ran around two sides of the room. Mahon half-expected to see a dwarf pop up behind the counter. Lucy was dragging on an El Cheapo and seemed oblivious to his agitation at not finding anyone to sell /serve him food and drink.

Out in the kitchen—which they soon found, beyond the room with the bar—they, well, Mahon at least, prepared some kai / food. Lucy contented herself with a beer from the chiller as she watched the gaunt stranger. There was plenty of food—just no staff or customers.

They ate in the 'restaurant'—Mahon voraciously, Lucy less so. Their conversation consisted of him burping and chewing and her asking "pass the salt, please."

Then it was silent, and Mahon asked "Are you tired?"

"No," said Lucy, "but I'm bored. There's nothing around—no music, no television, sweet fuck all in fact. I'm going out to see what I can see."

And she did, leaving Mahon alone, sitting by himself at the bar.

*

Te Neke was all fired up. He wanted his money— now. He thrashed the old Valiant around curves and flatlined the worn accelerator pedal until the shaky vehicle began to screech in complaint. From what he had been able to get out of Hemi, the remnants of the Tāhae gang had headed up north. 'Probably wasting my fucking money on piss and dope—the bastards.'

Carlos Te Neke had a firm goal. It had been a long, long time in gestation, but now—he felt deep within his soul—was the time to fire it into action. He wanted all out revolution in the skinny country. He had much of the finance already, but this latest hassle was slowing his momentum.

And his 'bosses' wouldn't be too pleased if they found out that their plans for action had been stalled by the very people Te Neke was fuelling the revolution with and for. He smiled inwardly—he was never going to tell these 'bosses' his real reasons for the rebellion until they were expelled or dead, and then it wouldn't matter. Te Neke had seen too many of his people in court, jail, nut-houses, factories, remedial classes, abattoirs, drains—insolvent and insulted—the list could have gone on forever. Te Neke had a burning rage inside him, an angry flame that lusted for retribution against those whom he perceived to be responsible for this inequity, this outrage, this massacre of his people's wairua. And they were not indigenous.

Te Neke had listened a lot to his Papa—who had grown up at a time when he was beaten for speaking his own reo at school, and who had been banned from the public bar at his local hotel because he was indigenous.

Things had been little better for Carlos: there was no opportunity to learn his reo—or language—at the city school he had been sent to—they didn't teach it. But he was shunted straight into training for the first fifteen, even though it wasn't his buzz to play the bloody game! He had been, and still was, sickened by the prejudice—obvious, and clandestine—that he had encountered because he was indigenous, and it was not from non-indigenous all of the time either. He was even more furious about his culture being utilised on convenient occasions by those non-indigenous who seemed to have no heritage of their own, but were more than willing to appropriate his. Thus the haka or war challenge, the manaia / taonga or bone carvings, the tattoo with the traditional motifs, were all now 'de rigeur' for many from a different Weltanschauung who seemed perfectly happy to claim them for themselves.

It was time to rise up and re-take the country, to restore an approach to life that had priorities very different to those that existed at the moment. A new language would have to be created to even begin to bridge the differences between them. It cheered him briefly to think that the world didn't need an invasion of alien beings—they were already here, en masse.

He also smiled because he knew beyond 'a shadow of a doubt' that he would succeed in his mission. He had the spooks' word for it.

Outside in the molten heat that melted the tarseal, a hungry hawk looked up sheepishly from the flattened dead sheep it was devouring.

Te Neke sped on.

FOURTEEN

Mahon didn't get to see Lucy again that night, and thus rationalised that he had missed out on the sexual adventure he had been lusting after. In his self-absorption he had omitted to think that maybe Lucy didn't want sex with him, and that she had her own priorities. Mahon's carnal thoughts were interrupted by the arrival of a guy who came into the bar and asked, nonchalantly, if Mahon wanted a drink.

Mahon was never one to say no to alcohol, so said, "OK," and soon the two were away laughing.

It transpired that the freckle-faced chap with the shock of red hair and flaming goatee beard was called Karl, and that he wasn't from around here. He was looking for someone and was making enquiries. Mahon didn't push him for details because he wasn't particularly interested—he was simply enjoying drinking the copious quantities of beer that appeared on the bar whenever Karl went behind it.

Karl soon got quite pissed and started to ramble on. He had once—he claimed—been a soldier, in some far-off place, so had a penchant for all things military. Mahon had also been such a trooper, but he suppressed that.

Meanwhile Lucy was outside, looking up. The moon was quarter-caste and the stars were obfuscated by clouds. It was a murky night. Lucy sat down and reflected. It was good to be out of Dirty City, but where to now? She needed time to think. She had no ideas, so decided then and there she would hang with the bearded guy in the big car and see where they ended up. He seemed harmless, if not a bit out-to-lunch. Still, Lucy liked speed, and the guy drove like a madman.

Lucy was lusting to hear some music so went inside and upstairs to find some. All she found were pieces of run-down furniture and a roomful of mannequins—the nude ones were all cast as Caucasians and had the same zomboid look earnestly trapped on their respective visages. She shrugged and carried on down the hall.

Karl, after a summary of all the great wars of the last five hundred years and a potted history of Genghis Khan, went on and on about the Hun and grapeshot and flak and Armalites and the Viet Cong and Martin Bormann and escape routes and Desert Storm and Tommy Guns and Commander Crabbe and plastic surgery. Chindits and the thousands of M.I.A. G.I.'s followed. "I mean, where are all these guys? They just don't vanish, man."

The guy was incorrigible. His tongue never paused. Raving and ranting he started on military aircraft, "Messerschmidt," he drooled, "now there's a great name, probably the greatest name in wartime aircraft. Magnificent. Perfectly crafted and designed. So well put together that it could damned near fly itself. The peak of mechanical performance. Messerschmidt."

Mahon had stopped listening and was drumming the fingers of his left hand on the bar, in rhythm with the du-dung-dung-dung beat reverberating in his temple. Mahon crafted amazing songs in his head. But could never recall a bar of them later. Generally these waiata were children of his dreams, but this time the genesis came during his awake, albeit drunken, hours. Du-dung-dung-dung, du-dung-dung-dung.

Karl had fallen asleep with his mouth open and was gently snoring.

Upstairs Lucy gave up on finding anything and fell asleep on an old couch that had been left in the passage, covered with year-old newspapers written in a language that she couldn't decipher. Curious how everyone is always sleeping.

*

Bobby Riley gently slid a vibrator in and out of herself and moaned along with the Supremes. *Baby Love*, sang Diana Ross, *Ooooooh, baby love* ... Bobby Riley smiled as she climaxed in delight.

Coincidently, not so far away, David Graham was jacking himself off into his computer screen as he searched the Internet looking for reviews of his book. He had stumbled—somehow—into a site called 'Asian Sluts'. One passage on the webpage reminded him of his early fictive endeavours: tomes he had penned under the rather silly name of O. Rang, before he had become an academic. He no longer wrote what now seemed to him such dross—which lacked the duplicit edge to be parody or satire.

David Graham himself was a satyr.

The inane look on both their faces was quite similar to that on Mahon's.

*

Mahon was the only one awake in the building. He wandered about for a bit before he too, succumbed to sleep, halfway up a stairwell, in a small vestibule with a couch.

He had a vivid dream that night, something about falling into a giant hole somewhere and then being discovered by a gang of black potency acolytes—Pangokaha—who wanted him to join them, and to smash the state free of Caucasian imperialist monopolies. Funny thing was, Mahon couldn't give a political brass razoo about white imperialists except for ripping them off whenever possible. As for monopoly—that was a game for residential fuckwits. Pangokaha played more lethal games.

*

Dr Dallas was still in his bureau. The telephone ringing had been a market researcher. He slumped back into his recliner as the rain shot down outside. He had anticipated more of a payload from the call. Maybe from his other, clandestine boss of bosses, who didn't inhabit the same continent as him, and who hadn't been in contact for what seemed like aeons. He plopped down the manila folder he had been skimming absentmindedly.

Dr Dallas was also the Commissar for the country. Very few knew this and none of those that did would have acknowledged it. Certainly no one in the current regime had any notion.

He anonymously gave to the masses glumps of patronising drivel, disseminated through the media in thin, once-weekly, rice-paper pap, and zappy, thirty-second television spots. He believed a lot of what he cobbled together too: about how the Indigenous were whingers who had to be watched and controlled; how immigrants were overloading the altruistic structure of society; how terrorists were rife in the rural races; how each citizen was duty bound to report anything suspicious to the correct authorities.

He hadn't altered his views much from the days when he had been a student at the Thoreau Military Academy in the big country, from whence he had been recruited all those years before. But he felt that the current regime, although aware of, and sucked in by some of his propaganda, were too damned slow to act on it—and had too many damned liberals and bleeding hearts in their cloisters. Too many damned Royal Commissions waffling on impotently. The situation needed a shake-up, but he doubted that the Suzerainty 'in control' had the impetus or the means to implement the required overhauls, given that it had been their damnably 'soggy policies' which had brought about the state of affairs the country was in, and now had to confront urgently — due to his machinations.

Even after the recent round-ups, there were still too many damned deviants 'out there' for his liking.

He pondered if he could really sanction more foreign — closet, or otherwise — intervention though. How long would it be before tanks rolled past his windows? Now that would be stretching his loyalties a little too far and fuck-up his imminent plan of retiring to a small lake in the country to fish for trout, in perpetuity.

*

I found a couple of pictures in my files that you might like to look at. They may have something to do with all this or they may not. I have no way of knowing and Wilfrid Sellars is dead and cannot help me. Here they are for your perusal:

Is this, in fact, Mahon? Rumour has it that it is. Taking a photograph of himself taking a photograph of himself into perpetuity. "Each man is the author of himself," conveyed to extreme latitudes.

What a fucking wanker I say.

If it is Mahon.

FIFTEEN

Lucy met up with Mahon downstairs in the 'kitchen', where—inevitably—he was preparing a feed of bacon, eggs and toast, which he had some-how discovered in the refrigerator.

"Want some?"

"No thanks," was her reply, as she scoured the 'kitchen' to find something else to munch on, and to drink. She finally sourced a bottle of orange juice and some slices of bread which she transformed into toast.

Mahon began to reply to Lucy's inquisitive questioning. Yes, he had had a variety of jobs in a variety of places, not only in the skinny country, but in other countries as well, including a brief stint in the big country as an exchange visiting professor. He had had to return to the skinny country earlier than scheduled as the guy with whom he had job-swapped had gone mad and proselytized Wilhelm Reich to the extent of stripping naked and painting himself in the colours of his own inner rainbow—indigo, orange and vivid chartreuse—before parading down the main street. Yes, Mahon had been married more than once, and yes, he did have children somewhere or other. Yes, he was once a musician of repute. Yes, he had had books published. Yes, he had worked at the university once as a lecturer in philosophy.

"I thought I remembered you," said Lucy, as she wiped the few remaining breadcrumbs from her lips. "Yeah, you were my lecturer for a while there—in Primeval Metaphysics 101." Lucy, had in fact never forgotten Mahon, and had always fancied him. Even after all these years, the red flash / flesh-point was still within her.

Mahon had all but forgotten about those times when he had been a popular, if not eccentric, university Don. He had written the well-known 'Doctrine of Ultimate Pointlessness', which had had its fifteen minutes of fame. Every dog has its day.

*

Lucy stared at Mahon for a long while, something playing on her mind, then asked him point blank if he had ever heard of Bobby Riley.

Mahon stroked his ample beard. The name rang a bell, so to speak, but he hadn't heard it for a long time. He would have to think for a bit.

He asked, "And what about you?"

So Lucy told him, episodically, her life story, beginning with her adoption out at an early age. Mahon listened, because as Lucy spoke, echoes from his own distant past came home to him as well. She felt comfortable and warmed to the task.

Lucy spoke of sexual predators, qua men per se; she spoke of her gender status, doubts and experiments, and of the women's liberty movement; she spoke of university and of Bobby Riley, of wanting her personal freedom, and all manner of things.

Towards the end, there was an interruption of sorts. A man, dressed in a checkered workshirt over a black singlet and sporting several days beard growth, sauntered into the 'restaurant' as if he owned the place. Which, actually, he did. He was the owner of Hotel Harold Holt as he proved when he gave both Mahon and Lucy a business card, somewhat the worse for wear to be sure, but indelibly one.

Mahon was about to ask him how come the place was open, but unpatronised, but Harold Holt only stated that he had to get back to his kelp farming business and that he'd see them again soon. Mahon shook his head and fleetingly thought that the world, or at least his part of it, was well-stocked with odd bastards.

*

Dr Cross was reading about spontaneous human combustion whilst listening to vintage Led Zeppelin pounding out on his giant home-theatre system when Kate McWilliam's tinny little car pirouetted up his hilly rural driveway. After their mutual warm salutations and his asking about her husband—a fellow veteran—and hearing her nondescript reply, Kate informed him that her daughter was sick. Dr Cross made small talk to the obviously unwell girl and gave her a deliberate examination.

Kate spoke of being on her way back home and made other small talk as the good doctor formulated some green liquid abomination on his cluttered workbench. The tyke had all the symptoms of a virulent strain of influenza. The malady served to silence the usually gregarious medicine man as he scratched his inner mind for clues and resolutions.

Puzzled, the Doctor asked Kate when her daughter had fallen ill.

"Last couple of days."

"Has she eaten or drunken anything out of the

ordinary?"

"No," here, there was a lengthy pause as Kate racked her reluctant brain, "but she did complain that the water tasted a bit funny. Seemed OK to me, though ... "

Afterwards, as the two drove bumpily down the driveway, Dr Cross' gimlet eyes noticed what turned out to be another paperback in the same mass Bonanza series—as advertised nightly on his wide-screen, latest-model, supa-television, by a recreated Hoss Cartwright—that he had earlier been reading, lying forlornly on his lawn, right next to where the car had been. Only this one was called *Inside the Cult of the Clitoris.*

Interested, he skimmed a couple of pages, standing there in the solid sun, sucking his pipe in, in avid concentration. Anything corporeally out of the ordinary fascinated him—he had been disbarred from general practice not because of incompetence, but because he delved into areas of medical treatment that his officious and conservative peers considered unscientific. He was, simply put, too radical in his 'holistic mysticism' to involve himself in the narrow and financially propitious collusion his peers enjoyed with the drug barons, grabbing Government subsidies for every petty prescription, and their obsequious 'kow-towing' to the decrees issued from the sober journals of tradition.

Those in the know, however, flocked to him in their droves.

*

Summary of similarities between Lucy and Mahon:

LUCY	MAHON
	Lost his virginity aged 15
Went to university and dropped out after a year or so	Went to university and did quite well. Ended up as an Assistant Professor, for a time.
Had a variety of jobs	Had a variety of jobs
Never been in the army	Fought and killed in an Asian war
Had a variety of lovers of differing gender bias	Had a variety of lovers: women of various creeds, colours, ages, sizes and motives
Caucasian	Indigenous / Caucasian cross
Never been inside a prison	Had a criminal record
Never been inside a mental hospital, except to visit	Had been a mental patient
Had been sexually abused by whanau	Had been sexually abused by whanau

Parents living in Dirty City. Lucy was born on a cusp	Both parents dead: Father died in his arms of cancer. Mahon is a Cancerian
Liked listening to Sade	Liked reading de Sade.
Generally cogent and articulate	Once cogent and articulate
Reasonably young	Older bastard
Didn't know where she was going	Didn't know where he was going
Believed in all things Occult, but merely dabbled in them	Had had a few experiences with kehua / ghosts, which had shaken him. Could be psychic. Could be psychotic. Or a mixture of both

The pair of mismatched figures chatted until it seemed a good idea to go outside and get some fresh air. But it was hellishly hot out there. Mr Sun was unforgiving and the skins on both of them began to burn.

"Too hot for me," said Mahon, taking his shirt off. He now remembered who Bobby Riley was—a gargoylic lesbian with a lisp whom he credited with the ruination of his first marriage—as if he had had no say in the matter. Now Mahon remembered why he had Molly stuck under the front seat of his Zephyr. He had been going to kill Bobby Riley.

He felt she had wrecked his relationship with her constant intrusions, cajolings, whisperings and inferences / interferences. She had even told him that his father had raped his mother—pernicious, sexist vitriol. He recalled fantasizing about driving to her house and blowing her away when she opened the front door. He was, he knew, heaping a tremendous amount of blame on the poor woman—attributing her with all the evil, shit, and insanity in his life, for his going off the deep end after the collapse of his marriage. We all need a scapegoat when we do not face the demon within us—Bobby Riley had become Mahon's. Even for things she could not possibly have done. Yet in some obscure, scarcely conscious way, he thought that through a showdown he might settle something finally. He shrugged. But did he really want to kill anyone again at this stage of his life? Perhaps he had lost the urge, the rage to do so. He stored the possibility away in his overloaded brain and looked at Lucy who was smiling at him from the shade of the verandah of the Hotel Harold Holt. She looked beautiful.

"Do you want to go upstairs?" He asked her.

"What?"

"Let's go upstairs and make love."

"Shit, you're pretty damned forward."

"Yeah ... well, it's too bloody hot to do anything outside. I don't feel like driving ... and ... and, you're bloody attractive."

Lucy smiled to herself. "Why not?" She didn't think she was going to see this guy again. Why not a one-day stand? Besides which, she fancied him.

They went upstairs and made love. Not fucked or screwed—made love.

Mahon was right and getting more right by the minute.

MAHON AND LUCY'S LOVEMAKING EXERCISE:

Fill in the blanks with the appropriate words:

Up there on the _____ they held each other for a long time, content to stroke each other's _____ before any disrobing. Mahon could feel his _____ getting bigger and bigger and he became uncomfortable with its size. Lucy, however, did not. He let go of Lucy and loosened his _____

Lucy took the hint and reached over and felt the sheer _____ of it. She caressed it for a while and took off her own _____

Mahon was excited by the perfect shape of Lucy's breasts. He dove down with his _____ and began to suck on them like the spoilt baby he was.

They both began to _____ a little and soon were deep in the throes of _____

It was very satisfying for both of them and after

131

their passion they both lay back and _____ at each other.

Possible answers at the bottom of the page.

Shortly before he snuck off to sleep, Mahon became aware that he was feeling better than he had for a long, long time. As if a gut-hot floodlight had switched on inside of him and he was slow-glowing.

Lucy waited until he fell asleep. She washed and left the building and the town. Time for her to move on.

Answers:

floor
hair
ego
mind
disproportion
shackles
tongue
writhe
lovemaking
glistened

SIXTEEN

One thing was for sure, mused a sweating, smelly Frances Xavier, he was going out tonight for a massage or two. He knew just the place to visit—a parlour down the road advertising cut price specials '2 for the price of 1' on weekday nights. Good for guys like Frances Xavier—broke at the best of times. Business was bad there too, since most people these days were in faceless Internet chat rooms, or, as a corollary—hypnotically ensnared in hyper-virtual reality porn sites, so couldn't be bothered with having their dicks actually sucked. No, Tessies would be fine: a little cossetting and corsetting, a whipping and a blow job would satiate Frances Xavier tonight. And he could finalise his plans just that little bit more too.

He sighed and turned on his solar radio and listened to some glib indigenous politician tell him that the time was now. The time to voice opposition. The time to unite for change. To kick out the overstayers. To expel the undesirable. Even though Xavier agreed with his sentiments, this upstart was an inappropriate fount for such views.

"You will be the first to go, you clown," smiled Xavier, as he switched off the tirade and climbed into the shower cubicle. He crossed himself soulfully as he pulled the curtain closed.

Appendix Two: Mahon's Dream.

A number of years previously, Bunny Parāone had been a damned good mate of Mahon's—during the times when Mahon had been his compatriot in the cells of one of the numerous judicial hostelries splattered around the skinny country. Bunny was a convicted murderer and a legendary gang leader. Mahon was transferred for far less nefarious crimes. Transferred however, because of his increasingly naughty behaviours—stories about which spread rapidly through the 'criminal fraternity'. Mahon by this time was already an underground anti-hero of sorts, a bit of a cult figure after the tales of his war deeds had filtered through. Some of us had also read his writings.

Oddly enough, they were also neighbours, years later when Mahon re-explored inner Dirty City and decided to stay there for a while—in inner, inner Dirty City. They lived adjacently: in crepuscular, dilapidated, wooden flats carved out from an ancient homestead. They drank a legion of beer together, almost nightly, and had so many stories to tell that it would fill volumes far larger than this one to begin to relate them to you. Bunny was no longer a leader of Black Potency. He was living a quieter life involving copious fishing, eating, and preparing home brew. He still packed a mean punch and his bulk had not diminished one iota. When aroused—especially after a session on spirits—he was not to be crossed.

Years later, when Mahon was at his most unhinged he had a vivid dream about himself and Bunny, among a throng of others, fomenting and then succeeding in a mass primarily Indigenous revolt against the extant power echelons ruling the skinny country—a cabal of businessmen protected by police and other uniformed militia. In the dream there was an ongoing war—fuelled by masses of firearms that the Indigenes had managed to secure by their never handing them over to the 'authorities' when directed to—for example during the frequent 'amnesties'—and by acquiring such-like from overseas indigenous groups who also viewed themselves as oppressed and over-regulated. The sad irony was that many of the armed forces were also Indigenes—who had joined up to obtain some measure of job security in a country that offered them precious little of such!

Somewhere along the line the Indigenes had been outnumbered and decimated. Bunny and Mahon, nursing their wounds, had retreated into a remote rift valley surrounded by impenetrable rock edifices. Chasms of stone so immense that the only way for the psuedo-imperialist forces to dislodge them would be by atomic weaponry—unlikely, given that too many non-indigenous people lived close to the zone.

For a while there was more bloodshed, particularly at the approaches to the giant rock bastion, but, becoming vexed and stymied by the crags, the inclines, the loose scree tumbling down at any time, and the shelterless barren range / rage of the landscape the uninformed, uniformed cowboys withdrew.

Yet, despite, and because of this isolation, the indigenous crew survived quite well in this massive sanctuary, so that over time the warfare abated to brisk skirmishes and occasional sniper-fire, primarily at the entrance to their valley. Eventually peace grew and the people of the zone prospered and relinquished a little of their desire to fight—put simply, their way of life was satisfactory. Their earlier inviolate desire for mana motuhake had contributed towards a war—now this self-same desire brought about its literal self. Tino rangatiratanga nē rā.

Crops were planted and thrived in the fertile soil watered by munificent streams that flowed from the sheer rock bunched on all sides. The Indigenes—all from different iwi / tribes—commingled and prospered. More stealthily arrived. Much was rudimentary—but food, drink and shelter were never a problem and their mutual empathies and tongue, their entire tikanga, more than bound them—it united them in one bond. Ko te kai nui te taima katoa nē rā: ko ngā tangata koa te tāima katoa hoki.

Mahon's final glimpses of his dream were of him fucking a beautiful wahine with long, flowing black hair and a moko—somewhere inside a verdant paddock surrounded by sweeping trees and watched over by birds. A brook babbled and the sun melted down above wild horses as yet unbroken and grazing on the thin stalks of grass. He moemoeā reka tēnei.

136

Thus was the dream. More of an after-image than a concrete entity. The images remained with him a long, long time. He smiled at the memory.

*

Mahon woke and recollected the previous day's events with some clarity and in some sort of chronological order. His brain fibres seemed to be slowly, but surely, re-knitting themselves. He lay alone on the bed and thought just how damnably 'nice' the experience with Lucy had been. He felt that some of his multifarious rough edges had been honed a bit and that something meant something again, although he couldn't say what it was.

Outside the room he could hear voices from downstairs, so he went in search of their source.

Harold Holt — or at least the guy who had earlier proffered the business card with this appellation on it — had a pair of large gumboots on (the wrong feet as it happens, the stupid clot) and was regaling a group of what looked like refugees about how to clean the hotel. He was scything a broom around in huge motions from right to left, and then left to right again. Mahon looked on for a while and then, shrugging his shoulders, strode over to his car. He didn't look for Lucy, for he sensed that she wasn't to be with him on the next leg of his journey. And there was something else. Mahon sensed that he wouldn't be at peace until he was with someone who shared his Weltanschauung. Only another Indigenous could do this. All the lovely Lucy's in the land wouldn't be enough.

For some reason, when he reached the crossroads outside the small township he turned back the way he had come and drove onwards and backwards, not using the same route as before.

He felt something inside of himself clamouring for attention.

He drove on, fumbling among his fusty-dusty music tapes for something worth listening to—John Campbell came on and blues-wailed Mahon for the next few kilometres. Then he died away and the long-ago recorded and over-dubbed voice of one of Mahon's children came on, speaking innocently of this and that. Mahon found himself with tears in his eyes, listening to his child. Another one born to face the quiet desperation. He was immediately transported back to a time when he had called in to see his kids. Or two of them at least. He passed a few tears at the memory, so vivid was it. He wondered, briefly, where his eldest daughter, Rangimarie, was these days. She had vanished overseas years before, "to find herself." It was her voice on the tape.

He continued driving until he happened on an atrocious scene. A motorbike rider had almost split in half a small, near-new, Asian car—light metallic green with red lights in the back window. The bike lay sideways, wheels spinning crazily on the tarseal while its swarthy easyrider lay yards away legs splayed at an inhuman angle, helmet dented and blood pooling on the road. Mahon slammed on his brakes and shot into the shingle at the edge of the seal. He clambered out and sprinted to the bike-rider whose leathers were ripped, whose face was pale brown, who wasn't breathing, who was dead, dead, dead. A broken soul on his way to who knows where. Mahon vomited, nothing came out, still retching he staggered over to the car, its engine running, water dripping out from underneath. He could hear dull moans coming from inside. Mahon tried to prise open the door to get to the woman slumped over the dashboard, groaning horribly yet quietly, he could not quite manage it. In the back was a small child lying across the dislodged seat, purple bruising on her forehead, legs collapsed beneath her, no noise, struggling for breath. Mahon threw back his head clutching for air and in doing so glimpsed a farm tractor approaching with a black-singleted driver.

The black singlet ran to Mahon cursing. They slammed open the rear door of the entangled wreck and gathered up the child's body, followed by the broken woman from the front. Mahon was so stunned he could say nothing—just did as he was told. "Go over to the farm, 'up there,'"—the farmer threw his hand towards a nearby hill—"and ring for help." So the Mark IV obediently shot over the rise and up the long metal driveway to the farmhouse, where Mahon dashed in, seizing the telephone as the wide-eyed farmwife stood by, drying her floury hands on a flowery tea towel. Then they both jumped into the waiting steed and sped back over the rise to the accident scene. Then they waited and waited, for an ambulance to finally arrive, and the steady men to place the shattered bodies in the back.

Mahon returned to the farmhouse for a 'cuppa', where the three-some avoided each other's eyes—they all felt shaky, bloody-sick and old.

They talked feebly about the way the skinny country seemed to be killing off huge proportions of its population via machines—often fuelled by alcohol. "No one does anything about it," said the farmwife, placing scones onto the kitchen table as the two men sipped their strong tea and silently agreed, wondering what the fucking hell was going on and when it would be their turn. The death-toll augmented every damned day like some jackpot at the races.

As day lingered on the heat wore at Mahon's patience—he journeyed aloof and alone, alarmed by the carnage he had witnessed. It brought him out of himself, squashed much of his self-obsession and vapidity—his otiose curve into nothingness. Contingency had rehumanised him.

He reminisced about his old mate, Sid McWilliams, whom he recalled lived somewhere around here. He had liked going to the McWilliam's place. It had been a real haven. Always a few kids running around with dirty faces, happy and outgoing. The McWilliams had tolerated his haphazard visits, fed and offered him huge wads of smoking dope that Sid grew out the back of the farm somewhere, amongst the gorse and the old car bodies near the bluff. Mahon smiled at the recollection. Yes—great company, great sounds, great dope. A couple of all-out parties too.

Things had changed though. Even Mahon had picked up on the discordant vibes in his later visits to the McWilliam's homestead. Tension, bickering, periods of sullen silence broken only by a kid's wail. Kate had certainly changed, had taken to moaning to him about Sid, something that she had never previously done. About how Sid never changed—how boring he was and how he took her for granted. And McWilliams was totally committed, obsessionally so, to his dope harvesting tasks. He spent hours and hours out there, wherever his plot was, and this no doubt contributed to the marital hiatus. Quite why McWilliams was so obsessed escaped Mahon, but perhaps, as in the cases of all workaholics, McWilliams was escaping from something—not facing whatever he really had to. Mahon had empathised with both of them, had been down that well-beaten path himself. Entropy seemed to rule marriage.

Mahon wondered how they were all doing now.

*

The hotel—if indeed it was one—was excessively dark and gloomy for such a bright day. Te Neke drew back on the cold ale with considerable pleasure. He had been told by the one and only person

141

whom he could find on-site, that yes, a chopper or two, maybe more, had passed through not too long before.

Carlos mused about his grandmother and the times that she had contacted the spooks. Or they had channelled through her. He was never too clear how it all worked. His Nana had spoken in guttural, masculine tones—her eyeballs wide, posture taut. She was no longer his Nana but some sort of spectral automaton.

"Ko ētahi tangata i whānau mai hai kaiārahi. Kei tō whakatakanga. Kāore whakaririkatia koe tēnei mahi."

So said the voice speaking through his Nana.

He had never forgotten the words which he took to mean that some are born to be leaders, and that this was his mission, which he should not ignore.

His Nana never knew this for she had fainted while the spook was talking. The spooks did that to a person. Came from another place entirely.

Te Neke was now no longer smiling sadly about the kuia, because after the second beer, he fell asleep. Someone, somewhere, had switched on elevator music in the background, and this had helped to lull him into a slumber. Besides, her words had calmed him, told him that all would be well. He had every reason to trust her too, because after his Mama had passed away from some white man's bloody sickness when he was just a kid, it had been his Nana who had been there for him.

*

Dr David Graham went into his campus office a little earlier than usual that day. He wanted to read the reviews of his new book and then anonymously pin them up on the staff notice-board. He also wanted to check up—in the esoteric section of the university library—on a couple of possible academic 'faux pas' that he may have made and didn't want to be seen checking up on. That wouldn't look good for a man in his position. Derrida was notoriously difficult to comprehend, and Doc wanted to convince himself that he knew what Derrida had been trying to say. Which was more than Derrida could say.

He smiled at the Island Indigenous cleaning lady who was mopping the vestibule of the library and crept over to the section headed 'European Philosophers'. He bent down to the subsection with *particularly obscure* scrawled on it in an undergraduate's hand, and picked out a tome, all the time picking at his left nostril with his free hand.

David Graham did not want to believe that he was no more than a piece of already written parchment, a hurdy-gurdy of others' used discourse and episteme. David Graham believed that he was more, far more than that. Hadn't he been published in all number of prestigious journals, worldwide?

He picked through the pages, and—after a few moments of slight doubt—convinced himself that he was correct in his interpretations. He rose to his full height and smiled. 'Ha.' His next book would be called *Rubbishing Rorty*. Or maybe *Barth and Barthes*.

As he turned his eyes to follow a twitching butt, he thought for a manic instant he glimpsed the back of a familiar head. He squinted intently through the masses of books, shelves and students. No, it couldn't be ... yet, it looked eerily like Fay Swine, just by the flab stretched across the shoulders, the short-cropped hair and the jutting ear lobes that resembled a large jug. Impossible—that bitch was long gone. Good. He did not wanted to be reminded of her at all. His memories of Fay Swine were of a grossly overweight, shit-stirring feminist who sweated a lot and had jubbering lips. He shuddered at the memories of their frequent altercations and her accusations of his 'chauvinism.' He peered again, but his view was obliterated by the floating population of people. He caught a final blurred snapshot of the psuedo-Fay Swine's back—thought he saw her bovine body wrapped in some amorphous spectral kaftan billowing towards the vestibule—then nothing. Whatever / whoever it had been, was gone. He paused to catch his breath, then headed towards his office to chat up Belinda Ungumbe, the African-Eskimo Muslim who specialized in post-colonial rupture. He would like to rupture her, he smirked to himself, as he eyed some of the fine, nubile first-years who were scrambling for the set texts at the main counter.

All in all, David Graham was pretty damned happy with life.

SEVENTEEN

I heard the bearded guy mutter something to me, but—partly because I was drugged or something myself—I couldn't make out what he was saying. He looked familiar, but the bruises around his eyes turned him into a pastiche of someone I thought I knew. That was the trouble with this place—the longer you were here, the more they tried to 're-edu-cate' you, the more alienated you became. Instead of being reintegrated, you disintegrated. That was of course, the whole idea.

I think he was telling me to 'hang on in there, effendi, because it wouldn't be long', but I can't be sure. I can't be certain of anything, anymore. Fact and fiction, cause and effect, true and false are all muddled up. I've been in here too long—I was the thirteenth 'admission'. I know, because the Doctor told me when he first interviewed me.

They dragged the guy away before he could croak out anything else and took me back to my small cell, too shagged to write any more that day. Oh yes, they give you pen and paper and limited computer access—with no Internet—how else do you think I've managed to jot all this down? I suppose they hope for self-incrimination. Most of this has come from what I remember when I was outside—the latest stuff is bits and pieces that I have picked up from others like me. Oh—and newspapers smuggled in on rare occasions. I'm more tired than I have been for a long time and I guess that it shows in my writing, eh. No time for being a silly bugger now, anyway, because from what I can gather things are heating up everywhere.

I'm hoping that this fellow I've heard about called The Snake hasn't been ratted on, and will somehow break us out of this fucking place. It's not so much the monotony, and the moronic questioning by machines, it's the growing / growling sensation that my existence could be over at any time and no one would know or care.

Things have gotten worse in the past few days too. I am again a focus of attention — getting hooked up to those damned 'truth machines' and their brachial voices. I don't know quite why.

I remember Dr Manhire and Professor O'Brien and their article about 'The Brain of Katherine Mansfield', something that I studied when Mahon and I were at university years ago, though our paths didn't cross. Something about being able to open the skull at any place and being able to pick up on a story that led on and back and around and through and into other stories, merely by probing the grey matter gently. There was no direct route. There was no primal source. Things didn't have to result from any other stimuli. There was not necessarily a resolution.

I feel my story here is the same. Everything revealed, reviled or revelled in — all at once. It doesn't have to make sense. It is life. Everything eating and fucking itself — an hermaphroditic cannibal.

Yet, from what we have learned about from Mahon, it doesn't have to be this way. That's why I want to set all this down as best as I can, while I can. If I ever escape this joint I'm going to find that bugger Mahon and try to get him to lead us out of the wilderness. I reckon his visions can be ours too, if only he could teach us,

I'm sure I just heard another dismal screech from down the corridor. The embedded electric sensors on the bracelet on my wrist are glimmering in the dark—thin multi-coloured wires dangling derisively, waiting to be connected again. Te Punanga certainly has a lot to answer for. So do those bastards who must have listened to that fat prick David Graham when he dobbed me in.

*

Ricardo Tubbs stepped out of the aeroplane into sweltering heat. Perspiration cascaded down his college-boy face and ran into his mirror-shaded eyes. He seized the white handkerchief from his breast pocket and wiped his eyes in a circuitous motion, all the time descending the passageway into the gizzard of the Arrivals Lounge. It seemed the air-conditioning wasn't working, for everyone was in the same boat, sweating and uncomfortable. It was the first time that he had travelled to the skinny country and his first impressions were that it was just another damned banana republic—like the scattered islands he had come from earlier in his reconnaissance trip, to 'check on subterfuge'. He paused to take off his double-breasted blazer in an effort to combat the heatwaves drowning him.

At one stage he had had to push his way past a group of uniformed police / security men—at least he assumed that they were such—who were batoning a pair of fuzzy-haired Island Indigenous individuals, right there in the middle of the terminus. Must have been 'illegals'.

'Fuck it,' thought Rico, he'd be damned if he would walk another step. Too hot. He flopped down into one of the sweat-streaked, psuedo-leather armchairs and waited for Crockett. There was no rush,

Tubbs was no longer a detective himself. He now worked for an ultra-cryptic agency run by one of the big country's most vehement xenophobic zealots. So secret was the body that it had no name, few knew of its existence, and he could not even prove that he was employed by it. It was a black hole, sucking in billions of taxpayer's funds, yet giving no indication of ... well ... no indication of anything, really.

*

When she had finally reached the marae she had been warmly greeted by her Auntie, who had cried out when she saw the marks on the girl's face.

"Aeee, he's been bashing you again, the bastard. Hell girl, I told you to leave that prick years ago. No good clown, that one. I'll kick his black arse if I ever see him."

"Don't worry Aunty, I'm not going near him

again," said Zita quietly, knowing full well that her Aunty Lolly meant every word. She was sweeping the floor now, knowing that she would be here for a long time doing mahi. That was OK too, because it kept her from mulling too much about Matipo and his wickedness.

It was a long time later when she saw that same hairy guy. Hell, he looked familiar. She watched him a lot that day, always aware that Aunty Lolly was watching her too. Chain reaction. She wondered whom he was watching. Everything was a domino waiting to fall.

*

Ned and Tuffy were all set to go and pick up some smoking dope when they saw the black Mark IV Zephyr hurtle around the corner.

"Fuck," said one of them, "haven't seen one of them for a while."

"Matiu used to have one, eh. He smashed it up good and proper one night after a party at Barney Ngarohi's. Used to go like fuck, though mate. He put a V8 in it."

"Whatever happened to Matiu?"

"Dunno. Still inside I reckon, after the scrap down at Boy Matipo's."

Then they were silent, for that scrap had escalated into a full-scale gang war and a couple of their mates had died.

Ned scratched at the scabs on his new tattoos and

said, "Let's go find us a Mark IV." So they jumped into their beat-up old Valiant and sped off down the country road.

Inside the Zephyr, Mahon had been thinking about dealing to Bobby Riley. Despite the memory only recently resurfacing. Wouldn't use a gun now though. Sorry Molly. He wondered if he still had that garotte in his car boot—he'd made it years before in a suburban steel factory when he was down and out and working for a living. Slick and silent.

"Nah," he mused, "waste of time." He took his foot off the accelerator, slowed down and gazed up at the sky. It was heavenly blue up there, clouds scooting across like slow dogs on acid. Mahon slowed even further and felt a huge load lift from him. He felt good. Redeemed. Relaxed.

He stopped the car, got out and sat down on the roadside bank. The clouds kept on and Mahon felt himself transported. He lay back, squinting through the munificent sun's rays. His tired and sore old body—well, not that old, really—humming in peace with itself. Fatigue and ache were sidelined. Repose.

Just as Mahon was drifting off an old car screeched to a halt in front of him and two guys— one dressed in scuffed black leathers, the other in faded denims, both Indigenous, both tattooed, one facially—sloped over to him.

Mahon recognized the first, taller one, straight away. It was his cousin, Ned.

Ned stopped short and swore. "Holy fuckin' hell.

150

Mahon you old cunt. How's it going cuz? I thought you were dead. Whatthefuckyadoinhere?"

"Cruisin' cuz, cruising."

Ned introduced Tuffy and they sat for a while, smoking a reefer so thick and redolent that Mahon became even more mellow. Someone turned on the car stereo and slotted in a tape. Soon the Isley Brothers were joining them on *Who's that Lady?*

Mahon felt the gentle warmth of the sun ravage his entire being.

They reminisced for some time before Ned suggested going up to the marae for a kai, as they had some mahi to do there anyway, and Lolly always had a boil-up on.

So they drove on up the road a piece to Whakangaromia Marae.

There was a working party going on and the three latest arrivals joined in—after the obligatory introductions and hongi. Mahon knew a couple of the kaumātua rāua ko kuia by sight and they related half of his whakapapa back to him, for they remembered his grandfather well. Everyone laughed a lot. Even Mahon, when they kept asking him why it had taken him so bloody long to get there.

Things went well this time. The weather stayed unseasonably hot and Mahon soon stripped off his t-shirt and joined in the gang work around the marae. The camaraderie was outstanding and the humour had him doubled-over half of the time, even if he was often the butt of the jokes.

They stopped for dinner and filed into the

wharekai mo te kai tino pai—after the obligatory karakia. Lolly had gathered her workers into a team 'par excellence' and had prepared nui te kai tino pai. Mahon—now, after years of doubt about his own tribal origins and an earlier feeling of whakamā around all things Indigenous—was comfortable in this setting, manifestly more comfortable here than he was in the 'outside world.' Yet, he was still aware of an internal clarion call to 'move on'—this inveterate restlessness forbade him from settling in any one place for too long, it would seem.

He chewed on his pork-bone, sucking away at the gristle, reflecting on how peaceful it was here, and harmonious. He knew that this wasn't always the case in such places and remembered only too well several miserable, acrimonious hui during his visits in the past. Still, today was sweet—tino reka nē rā—and he leant back as the speeches began. He heard his own name called out more than once, but made no effort to get up and kōrero. He just nodded and muttered "kia ora" a few times. Mahon could speak his own language with some skill, but today he was content to observe and relax, to continue to snap back into place. The waiata began and he noticed that it was the tattooed Tuffy playing a more than adequate guitar. He joined in on the songs that he knew, all the time conscious that there was more than one attractive wahine over by the kitchen making big eyes at him. He made no effort to encounter them, merely smiled in their direction when he felt their glancing. Trouble was, he also saw Lolly glare at them when they stared too long at him. Lolly was one of his aunts from one of his marriages to a lady of this iwi who had been killed in a terrible road accident. That had been some time after their mutually-agreed split-up, but Mahon was upset when he heard that the lady had died. He had loved her once—and in some way, perhaps—he still did. Then again Mahon loved all women, sometimes.

Mahon knew now that he didn't want to kill Bobby Riley anymore. He wanted something more important / constructive; he just didn't know what yet. But he also sensed that he would have to confront his nemesis before he could move on. He scrambled to his feet. There was some presence in the night sky that he could not articulate. A profound sense of 'the other' which he could feel within his bones. He knew then, as well as he would ever know, that there was something in existence that was intangible, irrefragable, alien. And that there were no words in any language to describe it. It had no presence in language at all. Here is a picture of what Mahon sensed that evening:

He struggled to find a semantic equation, a mor-phological resonance—some syntactic measuring stick for what he felt.

Nada. Nothing. Nil.

No words.

Tidak ada pertakaan

Kāore nga kupu

Ils ne sont pas les mots

Mei you walang salita

Somewhere deep in the bowels of the whare, some-one launched into a lament.

*

Later on, en route to Dirty City, Mahon remembered an obscure little book *The Haunted Woman,* by an obscure European writer, a tome that Mahon had read what seemed like a hundred years earlier dur-ing his stint at university. In it, the chief protagonist encountered a room where—when entered—he would receive the power to know things he had never previously known. The hero, however, lost the power as soon as he left the room; he was left with only a vague awareness that there was some-thing different beyond the ken. Mahon had had this same afterglow rankling in his frame.

*

Later, when she heard that Matipo had been

killed — "more likely killed himself on that bloody bike" — Zita Paraone was undecided as to whether to go to the tangi 'down country' further. She wasn't worried about how to get there — plenty knew him alright — but as to whether she could hold her head up again if she didn't go. It was expected of her, even if she despised him after the shit way he'd treated her. Mind you, there had been some good times too, especially earlier on.

He had changed after Sucker and his cronies had come around with big promises. "They were gonna get real rich man." Arseholes. Matipo had become more aggressive, domineering. Seemed to believe the hype that he was the 'hitman'. A kingpin. Zita had wondered where he got all his money from. And who those overseas guys in the flash suits with the funny accents were. He just used to smile his smile and say nothing.

She sighed. She had to go. But she sure as hell wasn't going to wail for the bastard. And as for all those bloody 'uncles' with their lascivious lips all over hers, giving the hongi — forget it. She would hide at the back somewhere if she could.

If they would let her — most of them still thought of her as 'Matipo's woman' after all.

*

It was humid and dark when the rusty Valiant sputtered into the front paddock — which was well-lit though, as the park was full of jalopies, battered trucks and vans, all with their lights on. A large crowd was sitting on seats in front of the whare kai—others remained inside their vehicles awaiting the body.

Te Neke knew that he had driven into a tangi as soon as he turned off the main highway and headed down the dusty track. The marae only ever had this many people for a death—day or night. Whose death he didn't know, until he saw the unmistakable form of Fat Man slumped on two chairs over in a corner, and—accosting him with suspicion—learnt that Matipo had been the victim of a road crash and would be "brought back home anytime soon."

"What about Sucker?" Demanded Te Neke, who hadn't quite figured out how Fat Man fitted into the equation.

"Cops got him a few days ago," sniffed Fat Man, wiping snot from his wide nostrils and stroking his massive paunch like it was a cat, "but I hear a couple of the boys got him out. Fuck knows where he is now, eh."

Te Neke looked at the colossus sprawled in front of him and pondered. This guy could be spouting a pile of crap to cover for his fellow gang members, or he could be straight up. Here wasn't the place to work on him though—this was not the occasion.

"Ever heard of Jake Heke, Fat Man?"

Fat Man was quiet for a long time, part of which he spent spitting wads of phlegm into the long grass.

"Yeah, I reckon. Real evil bastard. Wouldn't trust that bugger, e hoa."

"Where is he now?"

"Dunno, man. Dunno. Maybe headed to the city to spend up large." With that Fat Man closed his obese eyes and shut-up for the night. Carlos could get nothing more from him.

Te Neke wandered around for a bit. He knew many of the people there that night and greeted some warmly. A few were his co-conspirators. None were Caucasian. None were Asian. None were Eurasian. None were Negro. There may have been a couple of aliens, however.

"Kia ora e hoa," smiled one big guy Te Neke didn't know, "how's it going?" Carlos knew the man wasn't talking about the weather, but said nothing.

"Wait a bit, man, we can cross that river," was all Te Neke would muster.

Before the conversation could continue, the tūpāpaku / body escort party arrived and they fell silent.

Te Neke didn't see the guy again until—fleet-ingly—he glanced over toward the wharenui and thought that he saw him with his hands on his hips talking animatedly to Matipo's wahine, who was wearing shades in the dark.

"How had she gotten here? Who with?" Te Neke's snake-like brain slithered over the rocks of possibilities and ramifications. "Shit," he mused," I thought my schemes were cunning enough!" Who could he talk to? Who could he trust? By then, though, many had departed into the rural maze or drifted into the wharenui to sleep and join the truly departed inside.

It was really dark now, only a few stuttering electrical bulbs. They seemed to be winking slyly at Te Neke who chose not to respond and instead went into the whare to crash for the night.

*

Lucy was headed in another direction entirely. Back again into the 'normal', everyday chaos that is / was 'reality'. Pusillanimous passivity. A-rhythmic cacophony. Welcome to today.

She had contracted a cold during an intense rain shower hundreds of kilometres further down the track, and was sweating profusely. Great wads of sputum welled-up inside her lungs which she hoicked out in chunks of phlegm. She hadn't been taking great care of herself of late and her health was deteriorating fast.

She was also desperate for a nicotine fix, and accepted the first ride that day. The guy inside— a fair, green-eyed, handsome chap with fine Indigenous features who called himself Blake— offered her a smoke from his packet of Lord Lucans and she accepted—greedily drawing down the smog into her benighted lungs.

'Shit,' she thought, 'I'm a fucking mess.' Leaving Dirty City and then Mahon's big car / care, had begun to take its toll. She had escaped Bobby Riley, but to where? Her back hurt and she shook unceasingly. She wondered what had happened to that fella Mahon, and smiled weakly. Something self-ish emanated from him that made her feel that he would always hold himself for himself.

Blake took a few casual looks at the bedraggled, yet attractive stranger and quickly realized that she needed a doctor. She snored in a sweatful slumber. He shuddered as a wave of cold ran across him.

Trouble was, they were literally in the middle of nowhere, and it looked like more rain up ahead.

Copious persistent rain. A deluge.

Later on, they passed a fleet of trucks and elon-gated caravans going train-like in the opposite direction. Snaked over many of the vehicles were the words in big red letters 'Uncle Sam's Magic Circus' and as the entourage sailed by Blake was sure that many of the faces peering at their own were remark-ably deformed. Some seemed to have only one eye, others were bereft of an ear or two. He blinked a few times then shot a glance at his passenger who was fast asleep, reclining anonymously next to him, her right arm twitching and her breath panting in short, sharp stabs. His final after-image of the carnival was of an orange-haired man with freckles and a red beard, manically glaring from the back of the train.

Further on, as storm-clouds darkened the day, they encountered some lights. They slowed in anticipa-tion. Billie Holiday was crooning as Blake negoti-ated the car towards what looked like a police road block. A uniformed man with a peaked cap was waving a torch back and forth, undulating in the gloom. He motioned Blake to stop. Other officers milled around their stationary vehicles.

"Shit," snarled Blake, "what's going on here?" He hoped that his stash was well hidden. His worried tones were enough to wake Lucy as he wound down the car window through which the officer shone a torch directly into Blake's startled countenance, then past him and over the front seat, and then all over the empty back spaces.

Billie wailed on, caressing with her anguish.

"We're looking for an escapee," volunteered the uniform. His colleagues were still milling around up ahead, Blake and Lucy could not quite see what they were doing, but later—when they shared recollections—they had the notion that the uniforms were kicking and pushing something or someone into the back of a large gray van.

The uniform, finishing his search, let them back out on the road. No escapee here, it would seem.

*

Well before the sun had risen savagely over the horizon, Mahon had made his few goodbyes to the early morning kitchen crew and headed on his way. He checked under his seat for Molly, then settled back. Before long he came to a long, narrow, one-way bridge where he had to wait while an articulated lorry, which seemed extraordinarily high off the ground, rumbled over before him, its glossy black windows hiding its driver. The ground shook as the truck swept past and then the bridge was all theirs'—

man and car. He slipped Moby into the tape deck and turned it up real loud. There was more traffic now and the Zephyr had to slow frequently to negotiate the parade. Still, the rhythm caught Mahon in a seductive thrall, so he stayed calm and did nothing rash like swinging out and attempting to overtake every vehicle in sight.

Box-like houses appeared on the plains. Bands of schoolchildren grouped at bus stops here and there and the land ran out of cows. A police car eyed him suspiciously. Suddenly up ahead, a series of large billboards loomed over the highway. Most advertised new cars or overseas travel. He was struck, however, by the last of them. It seemed to be some block-letter aphorism. He slowed down and peered up:

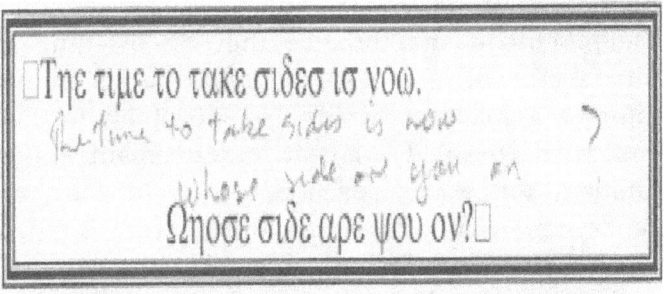

He was dumbstruck by this. Why—on the grimy outskirts of a grimy city—was this plastered over a fading billboard? He couldn't even read it properly. What language was it in? Mahon had no answers.

He put his foot on the accelerator and sped on.

The air began to pall and Mahon found himself winding up the grimy tinted window and turning on the air-conditioning. Moby rambled on. Dirty City's heart was pumping and Mahon gushed down one of its arteries, deep into its clenching, central orifice.

EIGHTEEN

David Graham was in his office, chatting rubbish to Belinda Ungumbe who rolled her eyes at his silly remarks about what he thought Edward Said had said. He then began to prattle on about Brassier and Meillassoux and their erroneous prognostications in the field of eidetic reduction. Belinda couldn't give a damn. She was only there because she thought that by listening to him she could score some bonus points in her efforts to gain tenure. So she listened gamely, feigned smiles and nodded her head in agreement. David Graham was an odious and sweaty little excrescence, who rubbed his hands together far too much.

She left David Graham as quickly and as pleasantly as she could, promising to visit again 'real soon'. Then privately fumed as she made her way to the Women's Collective downstairs. She brightened when she saw who was in the lounge—Esther, Emily and Eletia—the albino triplets—with their president Bobby Riley. Belinda relaxed back into a seat clutching at a silver chalice of cool white wine.

Bobby Riley was asking if any of the ladies had seen Lucy Whatshername recently, for she'd gone missing. The triplets feigned ignorance—they all knew that Lucy had grown sick of Bobby and buggered off.

Bobby was tempted to reveal a little about the links between the Cult and the Hon. Mr Sucker, about how there would soon be a sea-change in the land—but decided she could only trust initiates with that information. She said nothing about the minions out searching for Lucy. Bobby couldn't know that Sucker had no intention of ever sharing power with her, but then again, Bobby Riley didn't trust any males anyway, so had a Plan B.

*

The radio was playing Country and Western dross about broken hearts and lost loves when Jimmy Norcliffe switched it off. Daylight decaying into twilight around him.

Nearby was a low-slung brick motel—faded sign replete with missing bulbs. He drove into the small carpark, switched off the truck's engine and walked in to book a room. There were few patrons milling around, probably because the town was so far off the beaten track.

He was given Apartment 13 and went in and peered around. A cheap lamp, a K-mart eiderdown, a tiny colour TV and bugger all else. He lay on the

163

bed and rubbed his eyes. It had been an odd couple of days, or was it three now? He had forgotten. He had driven hundreds of kilometres, met some strange individuals, and was carting what he knew to be dangerous armaments to a distant warehouse. Quite who would pick them up wasn't his concern, although he had a fair idea, which made him worry about his country. Every-thing seemed to be on a downward spiral. The plug had been pulled out, somewhere.

Next morning it was raining. Jimmy decided to sleep in for a while—he could see no reason he had to hurry. He yawned vociferously, his head and stomach pondering breakfast. Fresh bread and sausages— their refrain sung. Oh, and tomatoes. Saliva formed on his lips. He climbed slowly out of bed— sore knees from too many rugby games for his province. Some sort of cartilage problem, or arthritis.

It was pissing down outside as he pulled his denim jacket up to his neck to avoid the naughty drips. He stopped in the doorway before sprinting across to the corner dairy. Outside newspaper headlines blazed *SUCKER PROMISES RADICAL REFORM*, as rain cried down the sheet.

Inside he picked out the food his body craved, then ran back through the rain, his knees aching. Inside the unit he cooked up a massive meal. Sliced up and buttered some bread, then devoured the entire repast. Afterwards he leaned back on a chair and licked his lips, closed his eyes and mulled over the day ahead. Driving around in this weather was not his idea of fun. He would take a rest.

He switched on the TV to see cartoons and soap-opera garbage, tried to concentrate but couldn't take it in. Someone knocked on the door. He padded over and threw it open. Outside was a bottle-blond woman with large breasts and faded blue eyes.

"Will you be staying another day, sir? As you only booked for last night, and the tenancy is up at 10am." She said this politely, without malice or rancour. Jimmy paused.

"Yes, I'll stay another day."

"That's fine. I'll make a note of that. Miserable day, isn't it?"

"Certainly is."

Their conversation sputtered on. Her name was Lily and she had married the owner of the motel "a cuppla years ago." He was a farmer, out in the pastures at the moment. She ran the motel, which, it seemed, was rarely busy. Not much in this district — just cows and tractors, ramshackle sheds and rusty iron gates. And, Jimmy reflected, an armament plant with a few out-buildings disintegrating in the hills.

Lily entered the apartment as Jimmy cleaned-up his dishes. Then they sat for a while as the rain beat down outside. She asked him if he wanted a percolated coffee. No reason not to, so they went down the passageway to the owner's much larger rooms. Lily lit up a cigarette and gossiped about the village, her husband who it seemed was seldom there, and the bloody Indigenous always demanding more land, more money—they should learn to shut-up and make their own living; should lock up the ringleaders and throw away the keys. Jimmy listened in silence, for he had his own viewpoints and empathies.

She offered him a beer and Jimmy said "yes." When she went over to the refrigerator Jimmy reflected that he liked the way she moved. He could feel his penis hardening. She brought him back a cold can and he drank deeply.

"You're the only guest still here," she noted remotely, folding up the newspapers left spread over the kitchen table.

"Do you get many?"

"Not a lot. Mainly one-nighters, on their way to the cities. More and more foreigners of late—not sure why. Nice men, well-dressed, always polite. They leave big tips too. Not much to do around here—except milk cows," she said, as an afterthought.

Jimmy grunted unintelligibly. Absorbed in guzzling beer.

Lily lit another cigarette. She brushed past Jimmy on the way to the lounge where she sat cross-legged on the couch. Jimmy appreciated the roundness of her breasts against his arms as she went by. There was a distinct animal ambience about her. He could almost smell her sex.

"There's more beer in the fridge."

He needed no further invitation to drink and went and grabbed another can, offering one to Lily as well.

"Why not?" she said, and rested back into her armchair.

"No, we don't get many guests around here" she went on unprompted, eyeing Jimmy as she spoke, words spaced out between clouds of cigarette smoke.

"Maurice, my husband, hardly ever comes here either. He is always out on the farm trying to stay one step ahead of the 'rural recession' as he calls it. Farming used to be the backbone of this country. Too many cheap imports now. Shouldn't let them in," she continued. The rain had stopped now.

They drank on and she made him a brief lunch of this and that. The atmosphere had become matey, two drinkers sharing little intimacies, reflections, opinions about why the country had crashed and what could be done about it.

Later, when they were doing the dishes, Jimmy Norcliffe turned to her as she talked about "those bloody Arabs in the rented farmhouse down the road," and placed his hand on her thighs. As there was no protest he pressed deeper, harder. She already felt moist as they began to kiss. Jimmy caressed her back, arms and breasts, but as he reached up under her blouse she pulled back and whispered, "Not here."

She led him to the bedroom, took off her top and her shoes and lay on the bed. Her breasts swayed as she moved to one side, her nipples already taut and erect, Jimmy—himself topless by now—sucked at them reverently. She moaned in pleasure as she clutched at his neck and pulled him closer to her. She was as horny as hell. He reached down and with her help pulled off her slacks and her panties and then dug his finger deep inside her; she moaned and stirred in his grip. They were tongue-tied, deeply enmeshed, as Jimmy struggled to free himself from his jeans. He rolled over, shoved them free, then rolled back on to her plunging in hard and fast.

Lily responded in her lust and soon they were pile-driving up and down on the bed. She was warm and wet against him as he rose to a climax, shooting violently and then less and less so; as the spasms dissipated she gripped him powerfully while moaning, her eyes half-shut.

Jimmy lay back, satiated. He placed his arm around her neck and she lay close to him, snuggling against his chest, soft and quiet. No need for words, no need for anything. Outside the rain had started again, drunkenly sputtering everywhere—here on the windowpanes, there on the spouting.

Later, they showered, and Jimmy made more wet love to her as the spray guzzled their bodies, Lily bracing herself against the wall as Jimmy entered her, his knees bent unnaturally as he thrust. The shower was an echo of the outburst outside which seemed to have exploded in earnest, lambasting down in great gouts, becoming torrential.

They climbed back into bed now and slept, bodies entangled.

As the day crawled on it poured down endlessly, hypnotically. Jimmy stirred a few times, but remained deeply dreamless. Lily woke once, looked at the man's tattoo and wondered who Joan was.

She heard the Landrover as soon as it hit the entrance to the motel. She knew that sound so well. Maurice had returned. She shook the sturdy man next to her—she had to do it several times before he woke, blinking stupidly as she whispered frantically, "Get back to your unit. Hurry. Maurice is back."

Jimmy thought that he was dreaming until she booted him firmly in the back—as he fell onto the floor he heard lumpy footsteps outside.

"Fuck." He fumbled around, grabbing his clothes, then bundling them together tripped out the bedroom door. Someone was moving around in the dining area. Jimmy shot down the passageway in the gloomy light, his naked body shivering in the inclement temperature. He found his unit and snuck in, wondering why he was feeling so guilty. Then he lay on the bed and smiled to himself. That had been a bloody close shave.

It was still raining the next morn when Jimmy paid the bill. Lily said, "Thank you, Mr Norcliffe," and smiled pleasantly. Maurice, a burly hirsute man said, "Hope you enjoyed your stay, mate."

"Sure did," replied Jimmy, but as he drove off out onto the highway, puddles splashing out from beneath his wheels, he reflected that well, maybe he had had good sex, but some of the conversation had brought him damned close to yelling at the woman. Shit, even he, a provincial boy at heart, shuddered to think of a whole lorry-load of Lily's illogical tirades.

Now he knew why he had felt guilty back there. When he'd been with Joan he had respected and loved her. Had never been able to partner up with anyone else. She came from a tribe way down the line. A staunch wahine that one. Jimmy had liked the whanau reunions, where he—an outsider— had always been made to feel welcome. He liked her family, even if some of them were a bit rough around the edges. He wondered where they all were nowadays, especially her wild younger brother. He smiled when he recalled how his brother-in-law had chopped down a protected tree, planted by some colonial oaf over a hundred years before. "Carlos, you bugger," he reflected, "must get in touch with you some time." He mused over how to do so, for he knew Te Neke was not an easy man to track down.

He thought a lot about his destination too, as he switched on the radio and listened to Patsy Cline whine the real truth. He rummaged in the mess of papers and permits strewn over his front seat to check that he could enter the warehouse without too many hassles from the gum-chewing bureau-crats down there. They always gave him a hard time.

The official letterhead proclaimed 'McBurgers: Official Sponsors of the Yachting World Series', and listed his heavily-bound crates as 'mall equipment'. What a global hamburger chain had to do with a consignment of what he knew to be small calibre weapons was not really a conundrum, knowing where the fast food giant had its nativity.

Jimmy Norcliffe pondered if he should even complete this run. Maybe it was time to make some phone calls. Someone else must want some guns other than some imperialist jingoistic goons. Shit—it could even be worth it to sell them to the rumoured 'rebels' that he had heard about over the truckie network.

He got down to some real earnest contemplation as the juggernaut clattered on.

NINETEEN

That night, sleeping at a mate's place on the outskirts of Dirty City, where he had stopped to quell his incipient fatigue, Mahon had a dream about Tamati, whom he hadn't encountered for ages. Something about respecting himself and the things around him. "He aha ngā mea nui o tēnei ao, e hoa?" Tamati had asked. "Tō whanau, tō whenua, tō Ariki, me koe," Tamati had also answered. That's all Mahon could recall the next morning, after one of the soundest sleeps he had had since he met Tamati, way back when on the beach.

Mahon's mate—Luke—wasn't around the next morning as he had had to go off to work in a factory, so Mahon shared his breakfast time with Luke's cat. Luke had been in prison with Mahon many years before. He was a convicted arsonist, but a good mate for all that. Hadn't burned down anything recently, at least as far as Mahon knew. He would

171

always have a bed for Mahon, "No problem, mate." Had even rolled up a joint for Mahon, but our hero had, "gone off marijuana," of late.

*

At the clinic Dr Rattnayasingha, who was a refugee from a desert war somewhere, gave copious medicine to Lucy and told her that she was run down and should rest up for a while.

Lucy—propping up an old umbrella borrowed from Blake against the squally wails of wind and sleet—ran back to Blake's car and clambered in breathlessly. Blake wasn't there. He had gone to bet money on horses. Horses were always racing somewhere in the skinny country.

Lucy lay back on the seat and contemplated her options, which weren't considerable. She gobbled down a couple of pills, plus a few more, to shut out the sickness as soon as she could and went into a hesitant slumber as the rain lashed the car and drove in through her closed but unsteady window, puddling itself on the rubber mat beneath her drenched feet. She had a fleeting query as to why Dr. Rattnayasingha was wearing heavily dark sunglasses inside his too bright building, but any answer was soon shut down by the soft gel that is sleep.

When Blake came back, munching on hot chips and tomato sauce, he took pity on her and took her to his mother's home which was conveniently in the same town.

His mother's name was Sue, but she was rarely ever home.

＊

Tubbs had waited for hours before he had given up on Crockett. He had dozed off intermittently and—waking abruptly now and again—shot a glance left and right, up and down the crowded concourse to see if he could see his one-time mentor and now freelance television advisor on Westerns, and sometime stuntman. No deal.

He shoved a cue card into the luminous digital-wallet shackled to his inner thigh. Images of diagrams and assorted odd-bods, flew out onto his sunglasses' viewing screen. He made out references to the 'Cult of the Clitoris,' and found a few contact numbers—though there was no guarantee they would aid him, as officially, he didn't exist.

He got up and made his way deeper into the cavernous warehouse that was the international airport. He may as well make the best of it, he surmised, even if his employment wasn't 'strictly legal.' He clutched the wallet closer to his person by tightening his upper-leg muscles. All those months in the gym had worked wonders for his self-control. Only Rico didn't seem to realise that he was dry fucking the very weapon that would screw him.

AFFADAVIT # 13: ROYAL COMMISSION ON SOCIAL DEVIANCE

... I remember hearing a gentle rap on the door. There was a pause and then I heard another rap — harsher. I opened the door just a bit — it was held by a strong chain anyway.

"Who's there?" I asked.

"It's me — Mahon," he said impatiently.

"Whaaaaaat?" I said.

"Mahon."

I didn't believe it. I swung the door open.

"I've just got here," said Mahon, "do you think that I could crash here tonight?"

I expected this itinerant sort of behaviour from him, even though I hadn't seem him in ages. He'll often turn up out of the blue.

"How's the kids?" He asked, as he sat at the kitchen table scratching his ears and rubbing his eyes.

I set a coffee down in front of him.

"The kids are fine. They're sound asleep."

"Jesus — how old are they now?" He asked vaguely.

"13 and 11."

Mahon looked tired.

I loved him once, many years ago, but I knew him well enough to never get back together with him again! He was impossible to live with, unreliable, went missing for days — even when he was supposed to be looking after the kids — and he'd spend

174

our weekly budget before we even got it. He'd keep the house awake listening to loud music and then tell us to shut-up while he wrote the 'country's greatest novel' as he put it.

Yet, he had given me his love for a time, shown it in many ways, finally though his unreliability and restlessness wore me out and our relationship broke apart.

I hadn't seen him for years when he knocked at my door, only heard vague rumours about him travelling round the country. Now here he was, half-asleep at my kitchen table, blurry-eyed and scrawny. I draped a large duvet over him and went to bed.

Next morning the kids woke him, arguing over milk and sugar out in the kitchen. They stopped when they saw this bizarre chap dressed in faded denims with unkempt hair and a shoddy beard at their dining table. Who was he?

They went over to him with their plates of break-fast cereal and sat down.

"Hello," the figure said to them. No response.

"My name's Mahon," and he reached out to shake hands with our son, the younger of the two, who finally responded by sliding his hand into that of his father's, and they shook firmly.

Mahon made a cup of tea and brought it back to the table. There was no talk then, just the clinking of cutlery on crockery and the slurping of tea.

"I see that you've met the kids, then."

"Yeah—reckon so." I waited for the jug to boil again.

"Do you want any breakfast?"

"What is there?"

"Most things ... well, do you want anything?"

"Yeah ... some bacon and eggs wouldn't go amiss."

So I readied us some breakfast while the kids finished up theirs. Finally, just the two of us were left after the kids disappeared, straight after their meals.

"So, why are you here?"

"Got a few things to settle."

I didn't push him any further as I knew he wouldn't tell me. Mahon never talked about his business affairs, so we ate, in silence.

"So when do you think you'll be off?"

"Soon. In an hour or two, if that's all right ..."

"Sure ... when do we see you again?"

"Dunno." A typical Mahon response.

I went over to the sink and began to wash up. He made no effort to assist me, just sat there violently slurping his tea.

The kids had reappeared by now, freshly dressed. Blake showed off his massive card collection and Mahon showed the appropriate interest. Then they vanished again—this time outside. I finished the dishes and went to get dressed. Mahon must have gone outside to find some clean clothing because I heard the kids stop skateboarding, and then the sound of three voices talking together, all matey.

He came back and asked me if he could use the shower so I told him to go ahead, and I chucked him a fresh towel. Not long after he made his goodbyes and jumped into his Mark IV in the driveway. We three stood in a small group and waved him goodbye.

As I said before, that was some years ago now, and years after our marriage was over. I later re-married to one of his former workmates and had another daughter—that relationship soured too—though for different reasons. Mahon has had spasmodic contact with our two kids since he left, they tell me when they see him. They have a bit of wander-lust too, maybe got it from him.

You know, when I think about it, he wasn't as bad as others in the Cult made out. Bobby told me that she had informed him that I didn't want to live with him anymore—she always acted as the spokes-person for us. Dominated us, I guess. That's why I escaped the Cult, until you guys held me here 'for my own good.'

— Sue Rua.

TWENTY

Mahon joined an early crawling queue whose tail was slithering its lemming-like way into the gassy entrails of Dirty City. The whores, the sweat, the violence, and the black mass of the granite buildings were waiting to suck him dry. Mahon detested it, and avoided coming here as much as he could. He hated subur-bia and the put-put-put of the army of lawnmowers every weekend. He despised the barracks of used car lots and the ranks of take-away bars lining-up on the forced march into the city. The endless series of traffic lights bewildered and disorientated him. It was as if the giant maw of the place slowly crushed him with its dehumanizing congestion.

Everyone seemed to move to the smoggy pell-mell of fast bucks and fast fucks. Cop cars patrolling. Politicians extolling. Poor getting poorer—and more desperate. Rich getting richer—and more desperate. Overseas visitors like a small gulf stream flooding through the downtown avenues. How many more people could live in this place before it exploded like some gross carbuncular? How long before there were street riots, plagues, open racial warfare? All these cars every damned day driving bloody miles into the city just to earn enough money to pay for the car! The spurt of newly-built suburbs of beige plasterboard, postage-stamp sections, manicured lawns and tupperware parties caused Mahon's brain to explode, "All this for a fuck!" Often only one fuck a month. And what about all those men like his Uncle Warnock who slept in separate bedrooms to his wife? No fuckee here, but still the poor bastard was lumbered with a mortgage that grew exponentially. The chase after the pink slot had ended up as a diurnal hell. The mirage of marriage.

All of the homes looked as though they had been built by the same man in one afternoon. The one mowing the lawns. Maybe he was mowing someone else's lawn. Mahon shuddered at the distant memory.

He needed a drink and he sensed that the Zephyr too was reaching the end of its tether. He spied a bar from afar as he and his car throbbed to a compulsory stop outside a massage parlour promising 'the best blow-jobs on earth.' They pulled over to the place of lubrication, parked in the grimy vehicular space, and Mahon melted out onto the pavement and through the bilious green doors of Hilaire's Wine and Bistro Bar Inc. The bar was quiet and under-nourished. A crumbling poster or two on the walls. A smell of disinfectant in the air. Phlegmatic drunks hoicking at one end of the counter. He ordered an ale and went in search of the men's toilet. He needed a piss real bad.

REDUCTION OF THE EGO:

I

J

T

٦

|

|

-

.

179

This was the first thing that Mahon saw—taking up an entire wall of the toilets. It took him a while and several beers to comprehend what it meant, if it was supposed to mean anything at all. Mahon took it to 'mean' that an individual should not attempt ego construction but should deconstruct to the stage of non-individuality. The One should merge with the All.

'Yep,' mused Mahon to himself, as he was the only person present 'post-modern mysticism.' Of course. It all made sense. Except that he was post post-modernism by now.

Refreshed, Mahon sauntered confidently back to his trusty Zephyr and started off on the final leg of his journey. He didn't require a sound-track, because the city was noisy enough. He found it difficult just driving in such a stupid environment anyway, without any further distractions. The whole place was making him hyper-zappy / snappy.

He headed toward the university.

*

Meanwhile, one of Mahon's children was waking up Lucy and telling her that she could stay for a while, and that he would try to source some more medicine for her. Lucy was semi-delirious by now and swimming in her own sweat. Blake had taken her to his mother's home and put her to bed. Sue wasn't around. Blake noted the palm trees in the living room and the arc light on high above them, but didn't give it too much thought. He had other things on his mind.

Blake needed to see a Doctor himself, too. His artificial limb was playing havoc and he needed a salve, pronto. He decided to drive out to Dr Cross' place to get some medication. Dr Cross had also known his wayward father.

As he trundled up the long driveway to the doctor's homestead he noted once again the bizarre collection of trucks, thresher machines and farm implements, new and old, scattered willy-nilly in the sunlight like abandoned playthings.

A Landrover was parked at the top of the drive. Blake pulled in beside it. As he climbed out a casually-dressed pipe-smoker strolled over and greeted him. Blake reciprocated before he thrust out his arm and blurted, "this bloody thing is giving me trouble again, Doc. Do you have anything for it?"

A puffing Dr Cross beckoned him toward the living room where he made a cursory examination. While doing so he rattled on about the perilous state of the nation, the weather and the crazy oriental war in which he had ministered to the dying. He was a gregarious fellow, but Blake already knew this.

"You'll have to excuse me Doc, but I've got to get back to town," said Blake. "How much do I owe you?"

"Got any dope?" Dr. Cross queried, after a quizzical look at Blake.

Blake obliged by digging into his stash. A fair swap. Real drug dealing—Blake thought later.

*

Te Neke had tried to chat to Matipo's woman during the day after the service, but he couldn't find her anywhere. Not even during the hakari.

He was about to leave the marae when, as he opened his front door, Tuffy strode over.

"Hey man," said Carlos," didn't see you around."

"Didn't know until a couple of hours ago, man. Uncle Tom told me he'd be running the service. Just got here. Bad one about Matipo, eh?"

Te Neke didn't answer directly.

"Have you got those guns and rockets yet, man?" Asked Tuffy, who was never less than direct.

"Nearly," replied Te Neke, "just getting together the last bit of cash. Got to find another contact, though. Last one got busted by those secret-service shits. Kāore ngā raruraru though—something's bound to fall off the back of a truck somewhere, eh."

"Yeah. Well, we're all ready to go. Just give us the word ..."

"Yeah, no worries. But the way you fellas work around here I better give you the word well before, eh!" Joked Te Neke, even though joking was the last thing on his mind. He paused and looked directly at Tuffy.

"Ever heard of a guy called Jake Heke?"

Tuffy laughed loudly, causing a few of the tangi-goers to look around, interested. "That prick. The Egg. Yeah, saw him a few days ago down at the pub. Bought us beers all night actually. Must have done a job somewhere."

Te Neke kept the obvious suppressed.

"Know where he is now?"

"Yeah—he got pissed and told us he was heading to the city to pay off all his fines and see the missus."

Tuffy scratched his head because Te Neke patted him on the shoulder and jumped into his car like a circus acrobat on uppers.

"Catch you soon," was what Tuffy thought The Snake had muttered.

Te Neke drove like a maniac. He would go and stay at his cousin's tonight, but soon he would track down that cunt, Heke. Had to get going pretty fast— lots of people were waiting on him, and that was the least of his worries. Those white foreign bastards would want to know what was going on soon too. Oh, he reconsidered, they weren't all white actually. How is it that the worst traitors are your own kind? Bloody double agents everywhere.

On the way he came across a police road-block. Te Neke gave perfunctory replies to the fat uniform, not wanting to be busted and all the shit that went with it: the driving to the station, the endless paper-work, the lawyer with the high blood pressure and the nervous tic taking notes, the night(s) in the cell with the drunks, homosexuals, drunk homosexuals, thugs, losers and misfits. Some people made crime a way of life, or it made a life for them —from 'crims' to criminologists—but it was a field Te Neke didn't want to get involved in. He already had more than his fair share of hassles. This time though, they were trolling for bigger fish, so they released him back into the pond. Little did the uniforms know that Te Neke was the shark.

TWENTY ONE

Mahon couldn't find a parking space anywhere near the university, despite his circling it for quite some time. His car was not built for a modern day, inner city. All the other vehicles appeared to be of Asian origin: small and bright, like tropical fish swarming over a carcass—pick, pick, pick. The bloody roads were so narrow and circulatory that the Mark IV almost had to bend in two to make any progress. Mahon wondered if the inhabitants of these boutiques and bistros sitting politely in the avenues were as prim and proper, yet as twisted and trifurcatory, as the cul-de-sacs they found themselves ensnared in. Increasingly frustrated and angry he started to take his venom out on passers-by, shouting at businessmen dressed in white shirts and ties and clutching briefcases with names embossed in gold on the outside for all to see. "Fuckin' wankers," blustered Mahon, despite the fact that not one of them could have heard him behind his closed tinted windows.

Mahon drove in increasingly wider arcs until he finally found an irregularly-shaped spot, deep down a cul-de-sac, into which he dove. He switched off the engine, took a couple of deep breaths, and stumbled into the humid day. Before closing his door, however, he reached down and fondled Molly again, as if by doing this he would ensure good luck.

Mahon was going to the department to see David Graham. David Graham had been a major factor in Mahon leaving the academic life a long time ago. He and David Graham had had fundamental differences of opinion, and Mahon had turned his back on the silliness of university life and headed to the countryside. Thus had begun his voyage to the spot he now found himself in. David Graham had been his boss. Mahon climbed the hill towards the department.

He scanned the staff-list notice-board in the empty corridor. The department had downsized considerably and there were very few names that Mahon recognized. He saw David Graham was still on the third floor, so began his slow ascent.

Coincidentally, or serendipitously, Bobby Riley was also visiting the department at the same time. She had come to borrow a book about medieval women philosophers from her mate Belinda Ungumbe.

They passed each other on the stairs. They didn't recognize each other—it had been so many years.

Five minutes later Bobby was lying dead on the street outside, run down by a stolen Diners Club van. A book entitled *Dark Age Women* strewn over the road beside her.

Mahon heard the sirens wail as he rapped on the door of Dr David Graham.

David Graham took his time answering—he had

been sound asleep dreaming about teenage prostitutes and bondage.

When the door opened and David Graham recognized Mahon there was an excruciating silence.

*

Lucy felt better already, though she had no idea where she was. The fever had abated and the rest had done her wonders. She craved a cigarette but couldn't find any in the house. Couldn't find any people either, although she did see a white cat. She switched on the TV as she rummaged through the kitchen drawers in desperation. Some documentary about midgets voting for a new President was blaring out. She finally found an old crumpled packet of butts in a plastic sack near the bin and lit up the longest one—she sat down to puff and think a bit. "Pppheeww," she spat it out after only a couple of puffs. "No bloody wonder," she grimaced, when she looked at the crumpled pack from whence came the butts: 'Jimmy Hoffas' designed to rot your lungs ten times faster than any other brand. If you wanted to terminate your existence real fast, you latched onto Hoffas.

She had no money, few clothes, and a chronic headache. She didn't want to live in any city right then, and she didn't want a relationship. She didn't miss Bobby Riley. She had a sister somewhere who was a rural consultant for a silage company. Karin, or K for short.

Outside, the downpour dwindled into a drizzle.

K's place seemed as good a place to be as anywhere else, so Lucy left the house and set off in search of her sister. Up above, in the distance, she could hear the whirr-whirr-whirr of a helicopter. She looked up into the molten mercury sky but saw nothing. A clear aquamarine firmament, free of clouds, had magically come of age, and the humidity was chronic. Lucy was uncomfortably hot.

She trudged on to the nethermost reaches of the township where the air soon became rank with cowshit and dust. No noise—except for the faint whirring in the distance. Lucy saw a narrow bridge up ahead, water bubbling underneath. She clambered down the clay to ease her parched gullet, and to rest a little. The helicopter seemed to be closing—but still Lucy saw nothing.

Under the bridge, the water looked cool, clear and inviting. Barefoot, Lucy plunged her feet into the numbing water. "Haah," she exclaimed in shock and delight. She soon stripped completely and gingerly crept into the stream. Becoming accustomed to the crispness of the flow she plunged her head beneath the water and felt herself waking up— becoming clean and complete.

The helicopter was almost directly above her when she rose to the surface. She shifted under the bank, hiding, as the blades whirred overhead. Squinting into the sun, Lucy could make out two uniformed men. One fat guy had headphones on and appeared to be searching for something.

Luckily Sergeant Schultz didn't see her. She wasn't a priority, but there was interest in her just the same: someone had informed on her.

The craft hovered for a few minutes and then rose slowly up into the ceiling of the day, until it was a mere speck on the horizon.

Lucy clambered back into the heat, shook herself dry, dressed, and was soon back on the tarmac, thumb out, hitchhiking on her own sweet parabola.

Some people live lives like this. No set pattern. No happy endings. Obscure. Anonymous. Unstructured.

Lucy doesn't know Bobby Riley is dead.

She's alone now, but a lot less dependant than she was.

She's wandering out into the country somewhere. Good luck girl.

*

"Mahon, you old bastard," is all David Graham could say, when he got over his initial shock. "How the fuck are you? I thought you were dead!"

Mahon looked at David Graham like he were a simpleton, and went over to the desk. Graham rubbed his hands together, as if he hoped to instigate a fire. Any more friction and he probably would have.

More silence ensued.

Finally Mahon launched into a diatribe as to why he was in Dirty City — "to tie up a few loose ends" — and why, more especially, he was at the university department to see Dr. David Graham—"because you are one of the loosest ends, mate,"—at which point the good Doctor began to get more than a little worried. Mahon soon worked himself up into a state of agitation and started to bring up issues that David Graham had long forgotten about, things like who really instigated the nihilist society on campus (and who had turned up hypocritically to its inaugural meeting); who had plagiarized whose work about Ortega y Gasset (and his connotations for the work of Gabriel Garcia Marquez); and so on. Mahon became more abusive as he went, to the point it seemed he might punch David Graham—whose heart was racing, mainly because he *had* filched ideas from draft papers written by Mahon, not to mention plagiarized one of Mahon's early wives, and had long been waiting for Mahon to show up and accost him over the business—in some sort of Malthussian equation, the angrier Mahon became, the angrier he became.

"Let's go and have a drink, mate, and cool things down, eh?" Was all Graham could bluster, before his heart gave way and he slid to the floorboards, at which point Mahon finally took hold of himself and called Emergency. They soon arrived and carted Mahon's arch-nemesis off to the nearest A & E, where, coincidentally, Graham's cousin Bobby Riley, was also being carried.

Strange how events of a similar ilk tend to congregate in clusters, Mahon thought. Two sirens in one flashing synapse of time. He vaguely flicked onto notions of synchronicity, but didn't have the mental space then and there to kick into determinism and free will and whether it was all some sort of signage or mere coincidence.

Somewhat surprisingly, Mahon felt better than he had for a considerable period of his more recent life. His pulse was not racing and he felt calm, in control – at peace within his vast array of inner layers. He wondered—yet again—what to do next. Bobby Riley had now to be confronted.

He turned away from David Graham's bookshelves—after having actually studied some book titles for the first time in aeons—and noticed a picture of the good doctor resplendent on the cover of a publication which was lamely lying on the coffee table. Mahon turned the book over on to its front and read the title emblazoned across it, *Why Derrida is Wrong*.

Funny thing was, Mahon didn't actually think Derrida was wrong, just hadn't gone far enough out from the other side. He biffed the book into the nearest rubbish tin and stole down the stairs back out into the furnace of the day.

Outside students, policemen and gardeners were having what appeared to be an altercation about who owned the land, but Mahon didn't need any of that particular crap right then. A dog was shitting on the lawn of the high court building a few hundred metres down the block from the campus and cars were playing skittles with centre markers in a vain attempt to get to the next set of traffic lights first. The streets of central Dirty City were stickily hot, muggy, meta-cosmopolitan. Massage parlour whores mingled with petty bureaucrats, dark-skinned basketball giants with epileptic dwarfs, drunken bums with faded hippies wearing soggy eyes. Car horns blurted out their sad refrains as buses ransacked the thin inner-city lanes. Weirdo figures in long overcoats skulked around in the background, some pilfering rubbish bins, others just totally spaced out, or from outer space. Skyscrapers belittled him and the neon lights were a bad acid trip. Everything seemed to have sped up. Alacrity ruled.

Time to move on.

The trouble was that the car was nowhere to be found and after scratching his head, Mahon realized that he had parked in an Erroneous Zone—as the flashing street sign intimated—and that he would have to trudge off and recover it.

TWENTY TWO

Unfathomably for him, and despite his earnest prayers, Frances Xavier missed the assassination target entirely. The huge BANG only served to obliterate a few fronds off a palm tree that waved high over the passing cavalcade, and—even more upsetting for the avenging angel—was almost completely ignored by the perspiring throngs of supporters, vagrants, police, pick-pockets, terrorists, attendees and street merchants below. A few had glanced briefly up towards where he sat uncomfortably balanced on a balcony in the musty old Metaphysical Credit Union Alliance building, but they either passed the sound off as a sick vehicle misfiring, or an electronic loudspeaker blasting static—the later which necessarily accompanied political processions nowadays.

The damned bolt had stuck yet again, just as Frances Xavier had had a head shot all lined up, and when he tried to un-jam the reluctant trigger he accidently fired a bullet upwards, into plant matter, rather than downwards, into brain.

Frances Xavier climbed down from his precarious perch and headed to the unisex toilet to wash away the shambolic camouflage of mascara and dun eye shadow he had purloined from his sister on his last jaunt down to her quaint little enterprise in Blank Junction—oh so many moons ago.

Little did he know, that the presumed target was not a living presence anyway. Frances Xavier had been so out of touch with contemporary governmental pragmatism that he was unaware that the target was a mere machine cunningly crafted to represent the vulpine victim—run by electronic synapses from a control centre far away. John D. Sucker was no fool, for although he had snowballing support, he also had his enemies. Although his policies were largely sanctioned by his would-be executioner, his racial heritage was not.

Frances Xavier trod through a couple of rotting verandah boards as he clambered away. On the other side of the thoroughfare at approximately the same elevation, Rico Tubbs snapped telescopic photographs at high-speed.

*

Up at Luke's suburban abode, Te Neke unwound a little. He spoke about his money being purloined by some fella he didn't know. He spoke about wanting to get things fired up, and that there were enough people out there now ready to swell-up and take over the country—to drive out the business men, capitalists and racists who had stolen their land, language and health. It was time to push for putsch. Te Neke sensed it would be a long, drawn out affair, mostly guerilla skirmishes, for there was no way the afflicted could win a head-to-head battle—but it was time to take sides.

Luke knew about the revolution. He had been one of the first people his cousin had talked to about the notion. He had his own doubts though, which he preferred not to share. He leaned back and lifted his arm skyward towards the flaming sun.

"Relax, man," he sighed, "have a beer for fuck's sake." Luke was tired, not only from his daily working, but also because he was getting a bit hoha with all these buggers arriving at random and raving away. The fact that his own blood was here doing the same meant little.

"Have a bloody beer, man," he repeated. Carlos Te Neke did so and shut up for a while. He couldn't resist asking about Jake Heke though.

Luke looked at his cousin. Jake Heke sounded like some fictional character to him.

"No, never heard of him. Are you sure this just isn't more pangokaha shit, man?"

"Na, I reckon he's dealt to them too," replied Te Neke, sinking another frosty ale. "Besides which, their bosses seem to have been whacked a bit recently. Hear about Sucker?"

"Yeah, someone said he is on the run somewhere. But who the fuck cares? It's his brother that I'm worried about. If that fuck gets in, man, we're all gonna get shafted. He's a fuckin' dangerous idiot. Real Uncle Tom bastard." Luke was getting steadily intoxicated, and loving it.

Te Neke was silent for a time after that. Hone D. Sucker was one of the financiers of the revolution who believed that Te Neke supported his whacko views. If there was arranged chaos and insurrection, Sucker and his clique would sweep in and take power—indefinitely. John Sucker didn't give a damn. He just wanted it all. Carlos also knew, that such was the precarious nature of the nation at the moment, that any loose cannon with a cannon could jump start the whole bloody affray. Just one man with one gun.

Luke again raised his arm—this time more shakily. "Here's to Nathan," he shouted.

Nathan was a fellow Indigenous who had destroyed a prime sporting chalice a few years back. A rich piece of silver fought over only by men. White men with money.

Carlos Te Neke had already switched off. His forebrain working on overtime. Utu running riot.

*

Sucker had enjoyed watching that naked white sheila bathe—from the cover of the plush vegetation spouting over the river bank. If he'd had time and opportunity he would have had a go at her. But that fucking helicopter was all over the place and he had to remain hidden. He ducked further into the water and let its cooling balm wash over every pore. Things had gone a bit wrong, eh, and he needed time to regather.

They wouldn't ever catch him, he reckoned. He knew too many people in this land—too many contacts who knew the code. And he had too much mana. He would wend his way deeper into the country and lay low in the vast regions where hardly anyone bothered to journey anymore, since the city had stolen all the generations. Pity about his bike though. Too obvious on the open roads. Too many sneaky cameras tied into that core computer system. Had cost him a fair whack to get that vintage Triumph too. He'd almost whacked the old bikie who'd demanded mega-bucks for it.

He would wait for his brother whom he reckoned would save him when the time was right. Him and his other escapee comrades who were also evading, rebelling, tricking, surviving and gambling in the outskirts of a land that was simmering away on the element, tarrying a while before the big boilover.

He wasn't just another dumb sucker by any means. Or at least that's what he thought. He plunged beneath the river's swirling eddies as the bloody machine soared overhead again.

*

Blake went back to his mother's home only to find that no-one was there—just a pile of frazzled palm tree leaves beneath the spot lamps. He placed his umbrella in the front porch and said "Fuck it," under his breath. Lucy had seemed OK—he had liked her and had wanted to get to know her better. C'est la vie, n'est-ce pas!

*

When Mahon finally found the council depot, after intimidating encounters with giant electronic billboards which constantly exhorted you to vote for John D. Sucker, eccentric automatic crossing lamps and street trams that ran on remote control, it was closed. There was a notice on the front door which was so replete with arcane verbal obscurities that Mahon—intelligent as he had become again—had considerable difficulty comprehending it.

He realized, after some interpretive time, that he would have to pay money / pingers / moolah / loot to the council, preferably via some electronic machine with slots in it. However, Mahon did not have a special plastic card with digits ensnared on it, so he couldn't go to one of these machines and release his car from the vehicle prison.

'Bugger it,' he thought, 'I'll have to find a bank somewhere and get some actual real cash out and then trudge off somewhere else to pay some actual real people.'

All of which took a tremendous amount of energy, for banks with people in them were few and far between. Mahon had to walk a considerably circuitous route and to ask several passers-by for directions, before he could actually release funds from his one and only account, this after proving whom he was, which wasn't easy as he had misplaced his special government encoded coupon with his make-believe photograph on it, long, long before. His spare cash was safely—he hoped—stashed inside the big Zephyr. Incidentally, because of the abundance of fecund dialects and the myriad haphazard mother tongues now rampant on the streets on which Mahon prowled, he had considerable difficulty finding anyone with whom he could communicate at all. There seemed to be a network of impenetrable verbal patterns at play in Dirty City these days. The babble of a babel. Things had changed since Mahon was a boy.

Ultimately, Mahon made his way to the council yard with a roll of bank notes and saved his car from a night in the cells. It started first time as was its wont and Mahon turned left at the iron gates and headed out to where he remembered Bobby Riley's place to be—in the spread-eagled inner suburbs.

Several times on the journey, he fondled Molly beneath him. It was time to confront bloody Bobby Riley, big time. He felt pangs of chilly trepidation as he envisaged her face on first sighting him after all of these decades. Or was it less? He couldn't recall the time-frame. He wondered exactly what he would do when he saw her. He decided to plan nothing, to let events unravel as they would. A subconscious marauder with evil intent was lurking quite savagely down there in his soul, rearing its ugly head and ready to pounce.

Ah! Here it was, Gaye Vista, smuggled untidily and obscurely into a secluded side street. Mahon turned his car's wheels inwards and pussyfooted it down to the far end of the end. Outside Number 13 he switched off the Zephyr completely and waited for a moment or two or three to collect himself.

Above—high in the hot sky, like an ambivalent UFO—the sun thundered down, and Mahon was conscious of the beads of sweat gathering on his top lip. He swept his tongue hastily upwards several times in an effort to lick away his own waste.

He moved quickly. Inside his pocket he carried a sharp knife.

He fingered the front door bell and waited. And waited. And waited. No one came out. No one seemed to want to come to the portal despite his frantic pressing of the button. He wanted right then and there to savage the fucking door, to smash it to smithereens, obliterate it once and for all. He wished to vociferously abuse Booby Riley, to torment her as he felt he had been tormented by her, to physically thrust back into her face all the perceived shit he felt he had once been dealt by her. He pressed his ear to the windows around the house. Nothing. Silencio. In his anticipation, he had cut one of his fingers inside the pocket in which he had thrust his weapon. He sucked his bleeding finger and pushed through the weak gate to spy out the back yard. He peered into the mute windows.

Waste of time. Nobody.

Mahon sighed, deflated. Bathos swept through him like shit through a sewer—that quick and that complete. He sighed again as he turned back to the front of Bobby Riley's home.

Out front was a taxi—red, white and blue — and someone was climbing out of it. Perhaps it was her!

No. On closer inspection the form was not that of Bobby Riley at all. Too dark a complexion, too buxom, too pretty. Too feminine.

Belinda Ungumbe wondered who the stranger was stamping his way towards her as she ambled up the front path to Bobby Riley's house. She looked querulously at him, from behind her shades—which hid her tears and her reddened eyes.

"Yes ... may I help you please?"

"I was looking for Bobby. Is she around?"

Belinda swallowed a number of times in an effort to stem the sorrow and shock. She didn't need this.

One of the women that she most admired was dead and Belinda hadn't yet had sufficient opportunity to come to grips with it.

"Bobby's just had a bad accident, I'm afraid."

"Oh, I'm very sorry to hear that," Mahon lied, "is she badly hurt?"

"She died. I'm here to pick up a few things ... I must go now. Excuse me."

She brushed past Mahon who felt a quiver of excitement—a mesh of elation, surprise and disappointment. He sucked his finger a bit, dawdling, then finally flew off in his Zephyr while Belinda Ungumbe watched him through the mesh of Bobby Riley's living room curtains.

She found the stash much later when she opened her deceased mate's wardrobe—thousands of new bills piled neatly together with a thank-you note on Sucker Enterprises letterhead.

Belinda glanced at her solar watch. Time to pray. She could just make the basilica if she departed now.

Time to think too. She could use that wad of cash and so could her church.

The only blood Mahon spilled that particular day was his own.

TWENTY THREE

Te Neke didn't sleep too well the rest of the night—too many untamed animals tossing around inside his skull. He tongued the dull floss on the inside of his mouth and felt the light stab into his eyes. Time to move.

There was no telephone at Luke's and Te Neke had to prowl around to find a box. The first kiosk he encountered at the suburban mall had the phone ripped off the wall, yellow pages flickering at him from the ground. The booth smelled of stale urine, and graffiti covered the glass.

'Do you want a good fuck?' Read one, 'contact Diane at 464-2123.' How?

He wandered back into the main thoroughfare, full of broken cash machines and fountains over-flowing with dead fish, food scraps and used band-aids, to find a telephone that actually worked.

He tracked down Heke easily enough. There weren't too many with his patronym in the phone book and after a bit of ringing around, Te Neke found his ex-wife who said, "Yeah, he was around a couple of days ago. You a mate of his?"

"Yeah," lied Te Neke, thanking the woman and placing the phone back into its cradle.

Driving over to the nearby suburb of the ex-Mrs Heke, Te Neke recognised a fair bit of the neighbourhood. He'd once spent some time there. State houses, broken Vauxhalls, bits of ragwort, lines of shifty letterboxes without lids leering at him, stray dogs with wolf eyes. Graffiti eve-rywhere. Fuck-all flower gardens. Skinny kids with dog's eyes. Erratic patches of long grass. Boarded-up windows. Oil stains on cracked cement. Nappies flapping snappily in the breeze.

In the pub, Te Neke ordered a bottle and asked the barman, who for some reason was wearing an eye-patch, if he knew of a guy called Jake Heke.

"Yeah," that's him over in the corner," nodded the man.

Te Neke glanced around to see a tall, densely-muscled guy wearing sunglasses, leaning nonchalantly on a dull and dusty bar-table. He seemed very familiar.

"You Jake Heke?"

The guy looked up from his betting slips and said,

"Who wants to know?"

"Me. Call me Carlos."

"Carlos ..."

There was a pause. Someone had sprung the chromed jukebox into life. A song from way-back struggled to be heard over the midday din of casual drinkers and serious drunks. 'Shit,' one submerged layer of Te Neke's brain noted, 'bloody Golden Harvest. Years ago. *I Need Your Love.*'

"Yeah. You know my cuz, Hemi. Hemi Parata," Te Neke said this as a statement of fact, not as a question, as he now remembered talking to this guy at the tangi.

"So you're Te Neke," replied Heke, wiping his lips with the back of his mittened hand.

"Where's my money?"

"What fucking money?"

"The money you ripped off Hemi."

The two were tense now, eyeball to eyeball,

except Te Neke couldn't see the other man's eyes. He was wearing the latest sunglasses. The screw-you mirror shades.

"Fuck off, man."

The fight was a good one. They were pretty equally matched. Two clowns from the same tribe smashing the living shit out of each other, first in the public bar and then out in the car park. It was only when Te Neke slashed Heke with a blade that it began to abate. Heke bled furiously from the gash down his cheek. Te Neke punched him again with his bruised fists and it was enough to end Heke's resistance. He went down like he was made of loose paper.

"Where's my money, man?" Panted Te Neke, himself bleeding from the mouth. He stabbed the prone figure in the other arm.

Heke squeezed his shattered hands into two balls and put them up in the air. "OK man, fuck. Here— in my jacket."

Te Neke grabbed the guy's blood-drenched leathers and pulled out a giant sheaf of bills. He snuck a look around at the few stragglers from the scrap, just to make sure there was no bastard going to have a go at him.

"Where's the rest?" He spat blood.

"No more man."

Carlos kicked Heke fair in the midriff. The groan was pure animal. Heke did his best to gesture towards a gleaming chopper parked over by the bar.

Te Neke sprung the seat over the petrol tank and

found another pile of bills clumped in a plastic bag stuffed deep into the frame. Looked near enough to him. Worry about counting it later. He stood to have lost a few thousand by the feel of the bundle and given the gossip about Heke.

Heke had by then twisted into a crouch and he was coughing savagely.

"Sucker's gonna get you, man. He knew you were a fuckin' wanker," was all he could muster.

Te Neke spat at him.

"Fuck Sucker."

He reflected much later on that this Heke wasn't a patch on his tipuna, Hone.

The long road home beckoned and he took off. Nonstop now.

Trouble was that somewhere along the journey Te Neke and the Valiant had to part company. The car refused to drive anymore and he had to hitch. He'd have to get another car he thought. 'Yeah, why not.' He had the money, and still had stowed away thousands that Sucker senior had specified would go towards the uprising. It would, but Sucker would be the first to be 'uprisen'. Te Neke remembered that he had seen a mint black Zephyr somewhere along his travels recently. Something like that would be the thing. Trouble was, there weren't too many of those left around now.

He snapped out of his daydream when he saw the driver, who had picked him up, unscrew one of his hands from a socket and begin to rub away at the stump, all the time staring out onto the seemingly endless highway and massaging the wheel with his elbow.

Blake listened to Te Neke for most of their journey. Much of what the rather intense guy said made a lot of sense—indeed Blake remembered his own father talking about similar issues over the years, on the infrequent occasions that the two had actually run across one another. Blake filed away the thought that he really must get in touch with his progenitor soon, for he reckoned that Mahon would be keen to join up with Te Neke and his claimed legion of men and women ready to die for the re-establishment of Indigenous supremacy in the skinny country. Or at least consider it. He was about to ask if the hitch-hiker had ever heard of his father but never got to it, because he was interrupted in his musings by, "Kei muri i te awe kapara he tangata kē, mana te ao, he ma."

Blake blinked stupidly for a moment as he took his eyes from the road to stare at Te Neke.

"Sorry," he said, "my reo is not too good."

Te Neke said, "I'll translate the korero e hoa. It's something like: 'Behind the tattooed face, a stranger stands. He owns the Earth. He is white.'"

Blake knew straight away he was going to join up. No question about it. What the stranger had been pitching he had known for years—well before any intellectualisation process. "Right. 100% right." He paused. "What can we do about it?" He asked.

"Well," replied a smiling Te Neke, having fired

himself up,"if we keep going this way there is a place we can go to spring a mate or two of mine ... ever heard of Te Punanga?"

The sun was just starting to blink wearily at them on the brim of the horizon, when Blake also smiled and said, straight out, "No, but let's go."

"Good. There's just a few others we need to see. Oh, and a few things we need to pick up too. Are you any good with guns?"

Their story has only just begun.

On the CD player King Sunny Ade was the man.

*

Frances Xavier unloaded his weapon from the back of the van, and, concealing it amongst the vast corrugated echelons of stacked eggs due elsewhere that day lumbered over to the rear entrance.

He cautiously craned his neck through the great wooden swing doors into the vast inner expanse of the mosque. After stacking goods on a counter towards the rear, he freed his 7.62 rifle with the bayonet salvaged from a long-over Asian war and looked for as many bearded victims as he could find. He hoped his weapon would perform OK today after his rudimentary filing down of its innermost parts.

Ah. It was what these newly arrived so-called refugees called their prayer time, they assumed their bowed, bent and kneeling positions, close to where Xavier was watching. He knelt to prepare the coup de grâce—the admonishment from a God superior to any these infidels would ever know. How dare they pray here with their alien destructive religion? How many of them were bent on some heinous vendetta of their own?

No other thoughts crossed the stodgy mind of Frances Xavier after this fleeting cognition, and none ever would again, as his flabby neck was garotted incisively by a slick tense wire pulled against and almost through it by the powerful hands of a black bewhiskered man called Ayahab bin Noham, who was the senior guardian of this masjid. A bona fide assassin.

Xavier's still warm and twitching corpse was dragged outside to the container refuse bin and dumped unceremoniously inside—under empty cartons once filled with Halal's Wonder Tofu. The lone gunman sunk further into obscurity. Inside the tabernacle no one knew what had happened as the mullah's voice reached an inhuman high-pitched C, which was heard for kilometres over the surrounding suburbs as it escaped from multi-directional speakers massed on the arc-shaped rooves.

Later, outside in the car park, a thin black limousine drew alongside Md. Ayahab bin Noham as he gazed eastwards, and, as the rear left window wound down, a dark brown hand encrusted with diamonds and gold rings slipped out clasping a large full envelope and then shook the executioner's now richer palm. The car glided away, the logo 'Fats Hashish' lavishly embossed on the side panels just discernible in the glancing sunlight.

Allah—it would seem—had spoken.

Tubbs meanwhile, high up a tree, was on his mobile tapping through gibberish numerics. He had a hell of a lot to report if only someone would acknowledge his existence. And the photos—so many of them! What a dossier he had compiled, and only he could decipher it.

He still had some missions to fulfil. There were a lot of complicated intrigues going down in this cacophonic city: all sorts of worrying cults and creeds. He tapped a message to his cartel coordinators on his phone, via a miniature keyboard skilfully attached beneath his left wrist, 'chiaroscuro' was what he sent in his dysfunctionally acquired imperialist lingo—when what he'd meant to write was, 'can you rescue me?'

When the bough broke under Tubbs' weighty cyborgian frame it caused a large commotion in the quiet suburban neighbourhood. Someone called the police who were soon surrounding the guy writhing on the ground. They arrested him as he had to be either a sexual deviant or an activist—they were on high alert given the location of the dome just beyond the barbed wire.

They bundled the gibbering Tubbs into the back of the patrol van and took him away. They soon found that he had no attestable identification. Didn't officially exist. He was charged with 'impersonation of a person' which carried a mandatory life sentence.

*

It was night. Silent night. Less than holy night in the McWilliam's home. Kate had come back "for a while." Sid McWilliams lay awake staring at the mildew sprouting on the bedroom ceiling. Kate was asleep as far as he knew. At least they still shared the marital bed. That's about all they shared though.

He thought he heard a scratching sort of sound. He listened intently. Yes, there was definitely something coming from outside of the house. He then fancied that he heard footsteps, muffled, sure, but definitely a dull tread over in the living room area.

McWilliams shuffled out of bed.

"Did you hear that?" Asked Kate, who was not asleep and had been staring at the same patch of ceiling. "Sounds like someone is inside."

"I'll check it out."

"Be careful." Kate meant it.

In the lounge the intruder was piling food into a schoolkids' carry bag that he had found hanging on a kitchen chair. He was hungry and his mates hadn't fronted up, as they had said they would—maybe the cops had snapped them too. He glanced around, and paused—someone was coming, fuck it. He hid behind the door holding a heavy copper statue of Buddha above his head.

Sid McWilliams didn't feel a thing. He lay on the floor, blood trickling into the worn carpet. The intruder listened. Nothing. Maybe there would be some money somewhere in this bloody house.

Fuck it again. He fell over a kid's bike trapped in the passageway. Hell of a noise. Bound to wake up whoever else was there. Already a light had gone on down the hall.

The food scourer turned and saw her. She had a bloody rifle, for fuck's sake. Semi-automatic. .22. Pointing at him like she knew how to use it. Real mean look. Bit of a looker. What to do?

"Hey lady, put down the piece, eh. I just want some food that's all. Not going to hurt anyone."

"Where's my husband?"

"Who?"

"You know bloody well who mate," Kate McWilliams could feel the rage rising within her. Her veins felt like they were pumping blood at warp speed. "What did you do to him?" She was worried one of the kids would poke their head out.

"Listen lady, I don't know what you are bleating about, eh. I'm just a hungry guy." There was no way out of this damned house except past this woman with the gun. She was bound to contact the law too. Sisters are doing it for themselves, eh. What to do?

They both heard the moans from the prostrate McWilliams and a sort of febrile stirring from the next room. Then a young girl appeared at another doorway, opposite, rubbing her eyes. The intruder bent down to seize a glistening strand of wire.

When the guy with the facial pinpoint tattoos lunged for her daughter with his makeshift weapon, Kate McWilliams fired, point-blank. Had no choice. Was never going to let this guy touch her kids.

He went down like an obelisk, writhed a bit, then was dead.

The McWilliams couldn't know it, but that act was another flashpoint for the skinny country. Another Indigenous ploughed under by a gun-toting honky—regardless of circumstances.

The irony was that the fraternal politician who stood to make capital from this shooting was himself a fascist, and a racist, who pandered to xenophobia and treated his own cultural heritage with less respect than those whose home had just been invaded.

So it goes. Another twirl of the cosmic baton.

TWENTY FOUR

For once Mahon knew exactly where he was racing his car to. A small church on the side of a hill, in a quiet suburb, tangential to where he had just been. A grove of green trees swamped the church and the sun shone down on it contentedly—the high white sanctum with the high white cross and the high white candles. Mahon was going there to make some mystic resolution, as though drawn there by some faint command.

The vestibule was nearly empty, only a midget or two hidden beneath the altar by the multi-coloured windows, a priest stood bowed before the chantry, and an old widow woman with her tongue hanging out like a rabid dog lolling at the back. No one else. Mahon knelt before the cross. He did not pray exactly—he let thoughts ebb from his head in a long cathartic stream.

By humbling himself, by breathing calmly, he hoped to find the peace of mind he quested for. He became quiescent, focused. He did not expect a super-natural communion—a divine response to his submissiveness—and what he found was a kind of spiritual steadying, spiritual solace. A flash of a larger picture. A recondite glint. He sensed again, more resoundingly than he had for a long time, that somewhere a 'perfect sublime but materially unknowable system existed ...'[1]. The midgets and the purple priest were still there when after quite some time Mahon returned back outside into the late-afternoon blaze. He sucked in the air like a child catching onto a huge gobstopper and paused. A lame dog limped by. The old widow inside the church died. Nobody noticed.

TWENTY FIVE

Actually it hasn't been so bad here of late. They've left me mostly alone after the last round of interrogations and 're-education'. The staff—such as they

---

[1] 'And renders both natural forms and the very values normatively associated with them (goodness, reason, territory, the value of life itself) meaningless.' Nash, Christopher. *World Postmodern Fiction, a guide*. Longman. 1984. pg 62. Nash is writing about *A Voyage to Arcturus* by David Lindsay.

are, as most of our surveillance is electronically monitored—seem preoccupied. The gossip, from the few spasmodic contacts I've had—for it seems there are not so many 'inmates' left here, for reasons unknown to me—is that things are coming to a critical point outside, and that they are going to get worse before getting any better for 'us'; that the administration is gearing up for an insurgency.

So I have been left largely alone to wander around my limited space. I've also heard through the grapevine that The Snake has not been fingered yet. I wait with hope and do my best to remain alert. Anything might happen in the skinny country now.

The guy with the busted eyes doesn't seem to be around anymore. He was no Indigenous. He was from overseas and sure wasn't a white man.

I've also heard that David Graham is in hospital, somewhere, laying like a beached cretacean attached to beeping machinery—with gross intravenous tubing sprouting from his various bodily orifices. He probably requires artificial organs of various ilk. Can't say I'm sorry for him, that cornucopia of concupiscence.

Sense? Nothing much is making sense. I wonder if it ever has. Anything might happen here.

The other night as I lay awake I thought I heard small arms fire from way over there, somewhere. Did you hear it too?

If I ever get out of here alive, I'm gonna track down Mahon. We need him. Not just my own people of course, but—later, maybe, when all the fuckwits are gone – mankind per se, I reckon. So I'll thank him too, because he's sure as Hell kept me going and he might just inspire us all one day.

Yes—I'm sure that was gunfire. I'd ask some of the others if there was anyone else around to ask. Even the old tap-tap-tap on the walls doesn't get much of a response these days.

Oh. I should mention that they came in and grabbed just about all of my files and manuscripts this morning.

PROLOGUE

Dr. Dallas picked up the telephone after its umpteenth pring, pring. The voice at the other end was mechanically disguised. He knew from past experience that it was the director of the big country's sleuth programme. The gist of the metallic message was that troops, armaments, munitions, money— "whatever you guys need down there," were available, no questions asked.

Dr. Dallas politely acknowledged the offer, placed the telephone back into its receiver, and drummed his hands on the grainy desk.

Well, at least now he had something to report. Something to justify his existence.

He reached for the other phone, the regular office phone, to make a local call.

Little did he know that his priapic Dirty City peer, Dr David Graham, was an inert lump of blubber in the local hospital ward. Nobody had informed him.

He also didn't know that the hospital had requested advice from Dr Cross, an old foe of his, who was a renowned specialist in tropical diseases. The hospital had been admitting an increasing number of patients lately for an acute malady reminiscent of 'sino flu'. Death seemed likely unless an antidote was found.

The ailment had not been seen in the skinny country before. How had it got here? And why now?

*

Luke was drinking beer from a flagon he had just bought from the local wholesalers while a black bluesman lisped in the background. He looked up when the Zephyr scrunched to a halt on the front drive of his home, splaying shingle left, right and centre. Mad Mahon was back.

Luke chuckled to himself. Bloody Mahon was always entertaining—whether a depressed form of social disease, a hyperactive gigolo, an intellectual flame or a drunken bum—or a combination of all these and many others. What would he be today?

They sat and drank beer until dusk. Mahon was sensible and mature, for once. Luke noticed that the man had a few scars that his shorn locks used to hide. Could have been from anything. War? Self-inflicted? Road Accident? Lobotomy? Luke wasn't going to ask. Mahon would reveal all in good time. Or not.

Luke intimated that he knew of a few—more than a few—people who wanted an armed confrontation with the 'powers that be', "not fellas like you and me, man," to restore some form of sanity and justice to the skinny country. They were armed, arming, alarming. The 'enemy' as far as Mahon could understand through Luke's inebriated articulation, were the owners, the bosses—the usual scenario of Mr White Man having robbed Mr Indigenous blind. Luke made it clear that he was of several minds—he too was of mixed racial ancestry, but "hey, these guys are serious, man."

Mahon listened to the spiel with interest, for he had long been contemplating a similar kind of thing, although for him, personally, a revolution in consciousness was what was really required—some messy internecine racial / class struggle wasn't his buzz. As the Aimless Drifter he had no room for it. If the skinny country was in uproar, where would he, Mahon, hide? Still, he stored away the few details that Luke dropped, for future reference. Mahon had come a long way of late and was now firing on more cylinders than his chariot. He had begun to re-experience events from his distant past, not just as memories and recollections, but as vitally lived events. He could taste the flavours, smell the scents, see the scenery of three or four decades past. He now wished to peruse the future too, much more than just the few glittering glimpses he had received. He kept his re-found talent to himself.

It transpired that Mahon was going to leave the

city environs soon and that he wanted to store the big Z in Luke's spacious garage.

"Need to shed my past," is all he would say about it.

Luke consented to the storage, it was no skin off his nose.

Here is the Zephyr still parked up at te whare o Luke.

The next day, when Luke finally got out of bed after the drinks session of the night before, Mahon was nowhere in sight.

Much later, Luke noticed that the big rifle that Mahon called Molly, was not there either.

PANUI

Kia ora taku ngā hoa. E mōhio ana ahau kei ngā haumi maha i roto i o mātou whenua tēnei. Kei he pānui tiketike mo katoa: i tarai mātou kia whakatukuna ngā hoa ki Te Punanga. Engari, kāore he angitu tēnei tāima. He pakanga tino nui ki ngā tangata hemo maha hoki. He toto i ia wahi. He rawaka o taku ngā hoa e mate ināianei. He pōhēhē, nē rā.

Kei taku Papa ki Te Punanga. Ka tohungia ahau ia. E pīrangi ana ahau he utu hoki.Whakararautia i ngā pū taku ngā haumi. Kei te tāima ināianei. Nā, te taima mo ngā whakapāpā/, kāore he kakari whakamua.

Maharatia te kōrero:

Kei mate a tarakihi koe, engari kia whawhaitia a ururoa.

Haere mai ngā toa

Hello, my friends. I know there are many allies in this our land. Here is an important news item for all.

We tried to release our friends in Te Punanga. But no success. A huge battle with many dead also. Blood everywhere. There are several of our friends dead now. A mistake, eh.

My Father is inside Te Punanga. I will save him. I want revenge also. Hold onto your guns my allies.

The time is now. Time for skirmishes, not a full-frontal assault.

Remember the saying:

Do not die like the tarakihi fish, but rather fight like the shark.

Come on, warriors!

Carlos Te Neke (The Snake)

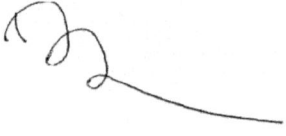